PUFFIN BOOKS

Zowey Corby and the Black Cat Tunnel

Gene Kemp grew up near Tamworth in the Midlands, took a degree at Exeter University, taught, married and had three children. She is best known for her Cricklepit School stories, which include *The Turbulent Term of Tyke Tiler* (winner of the Carnegie Medal and the Other Award), *Gowie Corby Plays Chicken*, *Charlie Lewis Plays for Time* (runner-up for the Whitbread Award 1985) and *Just Ferret* (runner-up for the Smarties Award in 1990). In addition are *The Clock Tower Ghost*, *Jason Bodger and the Priory Ghost*, *Juniper*, short stories, a poetry anthology, and writings for TV and radio. In 1984 Gene Kemp was awarded an honorary degree for her books, which have been translated into numerous languages.

Gene Kemp lives in Exeter with an elderly, evil-tempered cat and a lot of wildlife. Her hobbies include reading as much as possible, watching TV, exploring Dartmoor, supporting Aston Villa and Exeter, playing with her grandchildren and doing nothing.

Zowey Corby
and the
Black Cat Tunnel

Gene Kemp

PUFFIN BOOKS

PUFFIN BOOKS

Published by the Penguin Group
Penguin Books Ltd, 27 Wrights Lane, London W8 5TZ, England
Penguin Books USA Inc., 375 Hudson Street, New York, New York 10014, USA
Penguin Books Australia Ltd, Ringwood, Victoria, Australia
Penguin Books Canada Ltd, 10 Alcorn Avenue, Toronto, Ontario, Canada M4V 3B2
Penguin Books (NZ) Ltd, 182–190 Wairau Road, Auckland 10, New Zealand

Penguin Books Ltd, Registered Offices: Harmondsworth, Middlesex, England

First published under the title *Zowey Corby's Story* by Faber and Faber Limited 1995
Published in Puffin Books 1997
1 3 5 7 9 10 8 6 4 2

Copyright © Gene Kemp, 1995
All rights reserved

'Top of the City' (page 107), words and music by Kate Bush copyright © 1993,
reproduced by permission of Kate Bush Music Ltd/EMI Music Publishing Ltd,
London WC2H 0EA

The moral right of the author has been asserted

Made and printed in England by Clays Ltd, St Ives plc

Except in the United States of America, this book is sold subject to the condition that it
shall not, by way of trade or otherwise, be lent, re-sold, hired out, or otherwise
circulated without the publisher's prior consent in any form of binding or cover other
than that in which it is published and without a similar condition including this
condition being imposed on the subsequent purchaser

for Janice and for John Stocker School, Exeter

Ducks on the pond
Fish in the school
Whoever reads this
Must be a FOOL!

We're Cricklepit Cats,
    So – when you come to this school,
    Please raise your hats!

They fed me behind bars from an iron pan till
one night I felt that I was Bagheera – the
panther – and no man's plaything and I broke
the silly lock with one paw and because I had
learned the ways of men I became more terrible
in the jungle than Shere Khan.

Rudyard Kipling, *The Jungle Book*

Characters in the Book

At Cricklepit Combined School

Mr Frederick Bates
M.A., M.Ed.
(headteacher)

Mrs Thomson
(deputy head)

Ms Bellis (school
secretary)

Mr Merchant (teacher
and writer)

Mrs Merton (music
teacher)

Mr Percival

Zowey Corby
Hannah Fox
Sue Wong
Daniella Patroni
Natasha Smith

Also
Lucy Leadley-Brown

Naomi Perks
Melanie Burgess
Tiro Fleming
George Hopper
Matthew Brown
Roland Oliver

Black Cat Lane

Lilian Corby
(Zowey's gran)

Gertrude Leadley-
Brown (Lucy's
gran)

Gowie Corby
(Zowey's half-
brother)

Neighbours

Rosie Lee (a friend of
the Corbys)

Lorraine, Ruth,
Heather etc.
(Gowie's

girlfriends)
Marilyn (at the
supermarket)

And
School governors
Gowie's gang
National Front gang
Mr Martin Smith (the
Mayor)

Mr Edward Tiler (city
councillor)
Professor Fox
(Hannah's father)
Sergeant Price
Mr Tony Hopper

Ratbag and Blanket
(Zowey's cats)
Gowie's rats

Zowey Corby's Story

I'm Zowey Corby and I'm twelve. And no, I
don't have a middle name. Just Zowey.

Here's my address:

Zowey Corby
Black Cat Cottage
Black Cat Lane
Isca
Everyshire
ENGLAND
United Kingdom
EUROPE
The World
The Milky Way Constellation
The Universe
The Cosmos.

I'm glad it's not Black Cat Lane, Black Hole,
Black (alternative) Cosmos. For then it would be
completely different, wouldn't it? White Dog
Road? A 'No' Universe. That gives me the
shivs, so I don't think about it.

'You seem a happy sort of a girl,' says Mrs
Thomson, my teacher. 'Tell me your secret.'

'If I think about something horrible, then I put it away behind a curtain in my mind for later. But then I keep putting off later.'

'That's all right as long as it doesn't catch up with you one day.' She smiled at me.

I live with my gran and my brother, Gowie. Actually, he's a half or step (either is pretty funny if you think of it, half a Gowie or a Gowie in steps), I never remember which, though I can if I carefully sort it out. As you see, Mrs Thomson thinks I'm a happy girl and I don't have problems like nearly all the kids in stories have these days. I've got two cats instead, and Gowie keeps rats in the cellar. He's always done that* and still does, though my gran grumbles about them something rotten. Oh, it's quite safe, they've got cages and little wheels and things, and Gowie still plays with them like he did when he was a lonely little kid, before Gran and him and me lived together. He just lived with his mother then and she was horrible. She wasn't *my* mother. Gowie's dad – my dad – was in prison then and when he came out he reformed and that's when he met my mother. And there was ME. But his reform didn't last long and he emigrated to

*See *Gowie Corby Plays Chicken*.

Australia – I guess he was on the run again, but they don't like to say that to me – and after a bit my mum followed him, but I wasn't a year old and my gran had always looked after me and so I didn't miss them anyway. After a bit Gowie was in real trouble, so she collected him off his mother, who was glad to be rid of him, she said. Not a nice lady, that one. So Gran had us to live with her at Black Cat Cottage, and he stopped being wicked and is training to be a Saint, he says, though sometimes it doesn't seem much like it. Whew. I've got that lot over!

There *is a* problem. Because he was *bad*, he wants me to be very VERY good and I think I only need to be a bit good. So I have to stand up to him sometimes.

School's OK. The teachers are great really. Hannah, Daniella, Natasha and Sue are my friends. We're the Cricklepit Cats! And we're ABSOLUTELY FABULOUS!

Our school is Cricklepit Combined School and I suppose you'd call it ordinary – it is ordinary – but we do have something different: a tall tree in the playground. It must be a hundred years old.

The boys in our class are OK. They could be worse. One or two are actually *nice*. Especially Matthew Brown. I like him.

3

And two aren't. Tiro and Hopper. The Terrors. More later.

I love music best and writing stories, and I'm writing this one because we've got an end-of-term story competition and this is my story. I think I'll win it. But so does everybody else – think they'll win it, I mean.

All we know is who won't: Tiro and Hopper. And Lucy? What about Lucy?

It's Lucy I'm going to tell you about. It's her story really. Here goes. Keep your fingers crossed for me!

Chapter One

HEAD FRED IN ASSEMBLY: 'How do you have to
be to get to Heaven?'
CHILDREN (altogether): 'Dead, Sir.'

There we sat at the beginning of the afternoon,
as good and boring as sugar mice, all reading
our books in Quiet Reading Time. Hopper con-
centrated, tongue stuck out, fingers moving
underneath the words, tracking down the five
or six he knows.

It was absolutely quiet until . . .

'It's Silent Torture time,' Tiro hissed suddenly.

'What's the difference between Silent Torture
and Noisy Torture?' I whispered back.

'No screaming A-L-O-U-D.' He grinned and
whooped his crazy mad-parrot screech, making
Percy jump and say, 'No, Tiro. Don't do that!'
We're all mental in this class (even Percy, our
student, Mr Percival to you) but Tiro is something else. Beyond. Beyond belief.

Percy's supposed to sit and read with us,

5

though I saw him slide a form out from under his book, *Middlemarch*, and start to fill it in. He's done this before. Once I asked him why and he groaned and said he spent hours trying to catch up with what he should've done the week before and please, please not to tell anyone.

'They know anyway,' I said. 'All teachers work in Quiet Reading Time. They can't help it.'

'I'm not knocking it, Zowey,' he said. 'Everyone in the school silently reading, even the Head and the dinner ladies. A wonderful experience.'

Yeah, great. That is, if you've got a good book. But that day, the day I'll never forget – though I didn't know I wouldn't at the time, believe me – I'd got a book about this totally gross Sandra and how she learned to love her stepdaddy-to-be. A few chapters of her, her moaning mother and her bald, boring boyfriend, and I wanted to push them all in a lake, not that there'd be a lake near such twits, only a plastic puddle in a plastic park.

So, like Percy, I slipped an Argos catalogue from under Sandra's home life to suss out what I could con Gowie into buying me for my birthday. Something really WICKED.

Percy looked up. Suspicious creature.

'Zowey, are you reading your book?'

Cheek! What was *he* doing? But I pushed Argos back under Sandra and her mum.

'Yes, Sir.'

'Right. Well, five more minutes, everyone. Sit still. You've done very well.'

What Percy couldn't see was Hopper making a paper dart under the table. It was a terrible paper dart. Everything Hopper makes is hopeless. He can't even make a good paper dart.

I dreamed away the five minutes, wondering why authors don't write fabulous books. For kids. About kids. Who wants Mums, Dads and partners? They are *so* gross and stupid. Gimme, gimme . . . DANGER!!!

'Oh, come off it, Zowey,' says my gran. 'Get your feet on this earth!'

Why should I? Keeping feet on the earth and thinking about bills. Doesn't seem to do much for all those dead miserable grown-ups. What I want is a wild, dark night, the moon skedaddling through flying clouds, a tingle in the air, terror waiting behind the locked door, fear ahead at the end of the twisting path through the haunted forest, secrets, tombs, ghosts, a dark wicked raider, a mysterious castle and a doomed maiden! And a Knight on a White Charger. No, I'll be the Knight on the White Charger! Zowey Corby the Fearless, Zowey Corby the Wild Heroine! Moonlight – magic –

mystery – and me! Danger, beauty, romance!

And in walked Ms Bellis, our glam school secretary, long golden hair down to super-micro skirt like a little blue bandage. Tiro went down on one knee, as always.

'Out of respect,' he says.

'You just wanna look at 'er legs', says Hopper.

'GET UP, TIRO,' Percy said wearily. He's too nice. He can't really cope with Tiro. Only Mrs Thomson can and then only sometimes.

Behind her came a frightfully, terribly grand old dear in an Edwardian hat, a floaty dress, pearl earrings and a high nose with a smell underneath it (probably Hopper's feet). And behind *her* trotted our new headteacher, a wire-haired-terrier man, Mr Frederick Bates, M.A., M.Ed. – you can see it written on the board outside school. Everybody thought we were going to get a woman this time but Mr Bates came instead. And he's known as Head Fred.

'What d'you expect?' My gran grinned when she heard we'd got a man again. 'They would choose a man, wouldn't they? I knew they would.'

Madame High Nose spoke.

'They don't stand for visitors, then?'

'We like Quiet Time to be undisturbed. See

8

how engrossed they are in their reading,'
replied Head Fred, just as:

'Caw, git a load of that lot!' gobbled Hopper
in his awful voice, and threw his paper dart
straight at the old lady. Like the Queen, she
didn't flinch as it landed on her bosom. She just
brushed it off.

'Yes, I see,' she said, 'how engrossed they
are.'

Now our school uniform is the reddest red ever.
It's hideous, but then it would be, wouldn't it?
Though it's a wonder there isn't a law to say
schoolchildren must wear grey with convict
arrows stamped on it, ready to be punished for
the bad things they are about to do.*

So I make mine different. Grey leggings
instead of those skirts with soggy pleats. A
baggy red sweatshirt and lace-up boots and one
gold earring.

'My poor ole gran's not very good with the
washing machine,' I say if anyone complains.
That makes it OK. I can go on wearing the
leggings. But of course, my gran hasn't done
any washing for years. Her friends come round

---

*Kids are always wrong. Just admit it and shut up. Then the
grown-ups will forgive you and be nice to you. If you tell
them *they're* wrong – ah! Run for cover.

and do it for her while she sits drinking tea and doing crossword puzzles and organizing the neighbourhood.

I'm only talking about boring school uniforms because there we sat – all red and bright like sunsets in the classroom, just as:

'Git a load of that,' said Hopper AGAIN, in case anyone hadn't heard it the first time. Percy glared at him. The paper dart lay on the floor like a SIN.

'Children,' said Head Fred, 'I'd like you to meet Lucy Leadley-Brown, who's going to be in your class. Stand up and say hello to her.'

Madame Nose pushed forward the girl who was trying to hide behind her. She wore a long purple skirt, a purple blouse and purple tights. I looked to see if she had purple shoes as well but she had lace-up boots – like mine exactly – cheek! She had long brown hair, a purple hat, a purple cloak and she carried a purple sports bag. She was so pretty that Tiro had stopped peering at Ms Bellis and was gazing at her instead. Her purple and our red screamed at each other. I wondered if she was a Prince fan. No, it didn't seem very likely.

'The last of the ancient Romans,' said Tiro.

The rest of us stared, gobsmacked, and managed to utter, 'Hello.'

'We must all make Lucy really feel at home.

Naomi, you show her where everything is.'

Naomi is the kind of helpful girl who makes you want to stick out your tongue, wiggle your ears and shout, push off, get lost, go visit the penguins at the South Pole. Unfortunately, because they've got cloth ears and rotten eye-sight, teachers don't realize this and, as she rushes up and down wiggling, hand in the air, ever ready and willing and able, she usually gets chosen. And does it all wrong. And some-body else has to sort it all out. Here we go, here we go, here we go again. Naomi beamed hap-pily, like a frog, which I bet she was in an earlier existence. I was an Egyptian princess, of course.*

'We'll leave you, then,' said Fred, the Head, turning to go out of the door with Madame Nose. 'I'm sure you'll be very happy here, Lucy, with this wonderful class!'

This Lucy, this purple girl, stood staring at us, Head Fred's wonderful class, as full of fear as the room was full of kids, and as white as a shirt in a TV wash-day ad. I'd never seen anyone looking so dead miserable, not even Tiro in one of his blackest, worst moods. I could

*More about this later. I've got a super fantasy life when I think of the various people I've been. Only sometimes I seem to turn out to be my own great-grandmother.

11

see her eyes searching frantically round for ways of escape, away from us.

Naomi was burbling: 'I'll look after you. What a lovely uniform. You'll be all right with me. Haven't you got long hair? Let me have your bag. We'll be best friends, you'll see. You'll be happy with me as your best friend, I know.'

I knew I ought to do something about her, this girl who chooses boots like mine, just as I knew somehow they were the only things in that hideous get-up that she'd chosen herself.

Hold it. Naomi's Percy's choice. So don't interfere – let Naomi get on with it. And at that moment Tiro made his weird, wailing, crazy, demented, nutty, wild, mad-parrot noise that sets all your teeth on edge and is like nothing you've ever heard, and Hopper stepped forward and gobbled at her. After all, Head Fred had said to welcome Lucy and make her happy. Tiro was just making his parrot noise as per usual, but Hopper was making her happy. That's what Hopper was doing.

You've seen knitting after a cat's finished with it. That's how Hopper looks. Tangled, rubbished, horrible, like a battered toad. How could this girl, all in purple, upmarket and beautiful from her hat and her long hair down to my lace-up boots, know that Hopper's great, the nicest nutter ever, who only wants to cheer

12

people up and love them? (They usually run away.) He can't help the way he looks.

But at the sight of him she turned even paler. And if that wasn't bad enough, the room resounded with Tiro's parrot cry.

'Shuddup, Tiro,' I hissed.

Her eyes were so wide I thought her face would break. She dropped her bag, pulled away from Naomi and fled out of the classroom.

'Go after her. Bring her back,' cried Mr Percival.

Half the class tried to do so, and got jammed in the doorway. There was a pile-up. Bodies everywhere.

I stayed put. If that sad girl wanted out, I wasn't going to be the one who stopped her. Not that I thought they'd catch her. She'd got a flying start.

But I knew she'd be back later. I hoped.

Chapter Two

'Where do you find Hadrian's wall?'
'At the front of Hadrian's house.'

You come out of school, turn left and left again, go past the shops, Oxfam, the takeaway where my friend Sue Wong lives, the health food shops, the Kasbah, the Kentucky, the garage, the launderette and two boarded-up shops in the opposite direction to the High Street, then turn left again by the Black Cat and follow the alleyway down the steps, past the back of the pub and a shed. Then it widens where two rusty old bangers lie in peace surrounded by junk, Coke tins, yoghurt cartons and supermarket trolleys.

But then, right in front of you suddenly is a row of cottages overhung with trees. They have brightly painted doors, pots of flowers everywhere, mosaic pictures, crazy windowsills, mad doorstops. Cats sit on walls and steps and contemplate the beauty of life and the birds of the air. Opposite the cottages are tiny gardens full of roses, trellis, garden seats and urns, and very old trees. One garden is cemented over and has a Jaguar parked on it. Next door a motorbike's in pieces where Rory Bellis takes it to bits and puts it back together again all of the time. As you go further down this little alleyway, the trees grow higher, the bushes thicker and the cottages more hidden and blossomy, till it ends in firs, laurels, beeches and the Wild Patch, dropping like a cliff to the railway below, just before it goes under Black Cat tunnel.

Near where the path curves into the trees and bushes there's a short drive to high-barred double gates with big pillars. On the gates is fixed a single notice: ROTTWEILERS. Gowie put it up to keep prowlers away.

'But we haven't got any Rottweilers,' Gran protested. 'Only two old, tired cats and your rats in the cellar. And I wish you'd get rid of them. Nasty things.'

'That notice will keep jokers with funny ideas away!' Gowie said.

'Humph. In my day,' sniffed Gran, 'we didn't lock our doors. Didn't often shut them, come to that! What a world we've got today!'

'Yeah, your lot didn't make much of a job of it, did they?' he rabbited back. They often niggle away at each other.

I squeeze through a secret place in the

spotted laurel bush beside the gates and there they wait for me – *not* the Rottweilers, my cats, Ratbag and Blanket. Ratbag is a scarred, wicked ginger scrapper and Blanket is black, old, fat, furry, sleepy and full of comfort.

I sit down on the lawn at the bottom of our hidden garden and get out the can of lemonade I've bought on the way home. The cats wander round me and I lie back so Blanket can lie on me and fall asleep, zizz. The September afternoon's warm. Bees buzz in the flowers. Somewhere in my bag are some sweets, but I can't be . . . bothered . . . to . . . get . . . them . . . I close my eyes.

'I can't live here! You can't expect me to!'

The angry voice woke me up. Somebody was shouting mad. I shifted Blanket and sat up.

'Darling,' a woman answered, sounding old, irritable. 'We don't really have any choice. It's been offered to us very cheaply . . .'

'That's just how it looks. Cheap!'

'Well, I know. But the blurb says these are perfectly respectable artisans' cottages, built for railway workers at the turn of the century. The estate agent said some interesting people live here. There's a writer and a professor . . .'

'Don't give me all that. I don't want to know. They're just shacks. Look!'

16

'They have a garden . . .'

'A postage stamp. No room for *anything*. And this awful dirty alleyway. Full of cats.'

'It looks *perfectly clean to me*. It's all we can afford, Lucy. And we could have a cat too. It would make up for your dog.'

'A cat can't make up for losing my dog and my pony.'

'Oh, I know, dear, but try to understand. Please. I'm doing my best!'

The voice was familiar. I pushed Blanket away, crawled to the laurel bush and peered through the gaps at the bottom.

'But your best is awful. And you *talked* to that horrible yob with that bike.'

'If we're going to live here, let's try to keep on good terms with the neighbours, Lucy.'

'They'll all be horribly common, Candia says.'

Who the heck was Candia when she was at home?

But I'd realized who *she* was. Lucy! Of course. It was the purple girl, the Posh Git, as Tiro called her when he asked if she'd be coming back. That was a week ago. I'd written her off.

Now here they were, Posh Git and Madame Nose, on *my* territory.

I shushed Ratbag, whose mind was on food

17

as usual and wanted me to feed him there and then. He bit me. He's like that.

'We can't get any further this way,' the old lady said. 'We'll have to turn back. There's lots of lovely greenery here and I think it's the railway embankment behind these trees. You see, darling, it's not so bad. I rather like it here.'

'Yuck,' said Miss Leadley-Brown again, in a most unladylike way. 'The railway's all I need. Look! This gate says "Rottweilers". Rottweilers! What a lovely rotten neighbourhood!'

'At least it's a cul-de-sac. And it's quiet at the moment.'

'Oh, come on, I don't want to hang about. We'll probably be mugged before we even get to live here. Or torn to bits by Rottweilers! Come on, Gran, I know you're slow, but do try to hurry. HURRY! Let's get away from this SLUM!'

Not a nice girl, I thought, as I watched them go back up Black Cat Lane (its name). I'd felt sorry for her in school but now she sounded snobby and bad-tempered. I wouldn't dare speak to my gran like that. Funny we should both have grans and the same boots. I didn't know there were people like her. Not much else in common, though. She couldn't see how super-secret it was here. Stupid Posh Git.

'Come on, animals,' I said to the cats, and they followed me, wrapping round my legs and miaowing as we walked under the trees and round the pool and the fountain and under the vine trellis, through the conservatory and into the kitchen, where Gowie and my gran were having an arm-wrestling match.

Saturday was my birthday.

In new black leggings and top, wearing fabulous silver earrings, a box of chocolates beside me to dip into as I fancied, I sat playing my flute, shining silver, not the school flute I learned on but my own flute, at last. The notes were sweet and wild, blowing from magic worlds far away, singing of danger, freedom, beauty, strangeness, and my gypsy great-grandmother.

'I just hope that lot you've given her didn't drop off the back of a lorry,' sniffed my gran to Gowie, who was investigating a Dungeons and Dragons game. 'You can't have afforded all those presents.'

'Would I get Zowey mixed up in anything that wasn't straight? It's all perfectly legit.'

Gran raised her eyebrows. 'I hope I believe you. But I'll give you the benefit of the doubt.'

'I'd never hurt Zowey. You know that.'

I stroked the flute. I didn't care if it had been

captured from spiders on Mars. It was beautiful and it was mine.

'You give her too much. You'll spoil her.'

Gran had given me a book token. She believes in books (and tea and a glass of whisky).

'I didn't even get a card when I was her age. A kick in the teeth was more likely. And as for many happy returns! A laugh, that was. But I used to get myself another little rat,'* complained Gowie.

Gran snorted. 'I wish you'd get rid of those rats in the cellar.'

'I can't let *them* go. They're the last descendants of Count Dracula, my first rat.'

'Count Dracula must have been a female . . .'

'Doesn't matter what he was. I loved him. And he loved me. Only thing that did.'

'Oh, bring on the violins. The Sad History of Gowie Corby is retold once more. For goodness' sake, make a cup of tea, somebody.'

'OK,' said Gowie, and wandered off.

'What time are all your crowd coming, Zowey?'

'Well, we're going swimming first, then back here for supper.'

'How many will there be?'

*See *Gowie Corby Plays Chicken*.

'There's Hannah, Daniella, Natasha, Sue and me. The Cricklepit Cats!'

'And what do you want them to eat? If you think I'm making little cakes and spearing harmless sausages on sticks or jelly . . .'

'Sue's dad's giving us all Chinese takeaways from his place. Whatever we choose, he says.'

'That's generous. Who's paying for all this?'

'It's for free. He owes me a favour,' answered Gowie, coming in with mugs of tea.

'You've got it all well organized, I see. Any boys coming?'

'Course not. Don't be silly, Gran.'

'Oh, like that, is it?'

'Yes. Only Gowie's allowed.'

'I'm going out with my mates. Little girls' parties are not my scene.'

'Oh, please, please come. And we're not *little* girls! They'll want to see you. They all think you're fab.'

'Thanks a lot. But no thanks.'

'Please.'

'Well, I might look in. Don't count on it, though.'

Chapter Three

'We're Cricklepit Cats,
So – when you come to this school,
Please raise your hats!'

We rushed in, hair streaming, Sue Wong
clutching the takeaways, all of us shouting,
laughing. Gran was waiting for us, done up to
the nines and glittering with rings and earrings
and things. She likes a party, does Gran, as
long as somebody else does the work. I put on
my new CD and we tucked in and at last Gran
brought out the cake, with iced white towers
like a Disney castle and candles on the top.

'Did you make it?' Natasha asked.

'Well . . .' began Gran.

'Course not. She's never baked a thing in her
life,' I said.

'No, but I organized somebody else to make
it!'

'It's so beautiful,' Daniella said.

'Too beautiful to cut.'

'Where did you get it?'

'Ah, that would be telling.'

'Please tell us where you got it.'

'OK. It was from . . .'

The door burst open and there stood Tiro, framed in the doorway like a painting of a black thundercloud, Hopper peering over his head behind him.

Quick as a flash, I tried to jam the door.

'Out – out – out,' I yelled.

Fat tears blabbed down Hopper's face. Tiro's eyes were slits of blue glass. But Tiro never looks at you. And you never look into Tiro's eyes, because you're scared of what you might see there.

'You – didn't – invite – us.'

'Of course we didn't. We're not stoopid. Don't you be. We never invite boys. And if we did, we wouldn't invite you two. Besides, you don't invite us to anything, do you?'

But I couldn't hold them back as they pushed into the room.

'Oh, no . . .'

'Go away . . .'

'You're spoiling it . . .'

'We don't want you . . .'

Gran stood up as tall as five-foot-nothing lets her.

'Now get out, you boys. You're not wanted here. I'm sorry, but just go.'

Hopper held out his hands to her and gobbled.

'What's he saying?'

'It's his birthday too,' hissed Tiro. 'You know, other people have birthdays as well as Zowey Corby – but they don't matter, do they?'

'If you come in,' said my gran, 'then you behave. Promise.

'Oh, yeah. We promise.' Tiro smiled.

Gran divided her takeaway between them. Hopper gobbled his down. Not a pretty eater. I watched Tiro. I didn't trust him even if Gran did. I'd known him for too long.

'And now the cake! Zowey! Happy birthday!'

'And Hopper,' Tiro shouted.

'Happy birthday, Zowey. Blow out the candles!'

Hopper lurched forward.

'I want to do them by myself,' I cried.

'Big of you,' Tiro sneered. 'Generous girl, our Zowey. But, then, you can be when you've got everything.'

'Shut up, Tiro.'

I blew. They all went out but one and quick as lightning, only it was the opposite, Tiro blew it out.

'Happy birthday to you!
Happy birthday to you!
Happy birthday, dear Zowey!

Happy birthday to you!'

Hopper was singing 'Squashed Tomatoes and Stew' over and over – the only words he knows, I suppose.

I cut the cake into bits and we stood munching. It was slishus.

'If we'd known you'd turn up, I'd've asked Felix and Henry . . .'

'And Christopher . . .'

'Tiro's the handsomest,' grinned Daniella, batting her eyelashes. Daniella's richer than rich – holidays in Florida (Disneyland), winter skiing, a home like a palace – you name it, she's got it, and she's beautiful and brilliant.

Keep away from Tiro, I was just going to say, when Gowie came in. (I knew he would. He *likes* girls fancying him.)

'Happy birthday, Zowey. Hello, girls,' he cried, and then saw Tiro. His face changed.

'What you doing here? I said I wouldn't have you in here, didn't I?'

'He's been all right,' Gran put in. 'And it is Hopper's birthday too. And you didn't get *anything*, did you, Hopper?'

'Nuffink. Nuffink at all.'

'I gave you something,' said Tiro.

'I didn't like that chewing gum. You put somefink 'orrible on it. Poison, I suppose.'

'Well, have another slice of cake, then get lost, you two.' Gowie frowned.

We pushed back the rugs and started to dance, and as the boys started to go, Gowie suddenly grabbed Tiro and bent his hand over. Gran's watch dropped out of it.

'I left that on the cupboard,' she cried.

'Out,' cried Gowie. 'You just go . . . before I . . .'

But at that moment a black and beautiful, very tall, very thin girl came through the door.

'No, don't hurt him,' she cried. 'Tiro, Tiro, what are you doing now?'

'Nicking my watch,' said Gran. 'I left it on the side. But let's forget it now. Take that look off your face, Gowie. You were like him once.'

'No, I wasn't. I was bad, but not crazy like him. And I didn't steal things out of my friends' houses.'

'That's 'cos you didn't have any,' laughed the tall black girl, showing rows of white teeth. 'Not till I came along. Come on, let's enjoy ourselves. It's Zowey's birthday.'

'You boys can stay. But if you put a foot wrong . . .'

'I wouldn't stay here if you paid me. I'll do what I want. Stuff you, Gowie Corby. Come on, Hopper. Let's leave this bunch of brain-deaders,' shouted Tiro.

'OUT! GET OUT!!!' yelled Gowie.

They ran.

'Don't be upset, Zowey,' said Hannah.

'I'm not. I gave up being upset about Tiro ages ago.'

'Happy birthday, Zowey.' Rosie Lee, the tall black girl, and the person I love best except for my gran and Gowie, bent down and kissed me. 'I'll go and see Hopper later and take him something,' she said. 'Since it's his birthday.'

'What did you bring *me*?'

'No material possessions. I'm no material girl!'

'Yes. But what? Where is it?'

'Come outside. I've brought you a little tree. Your own tree. It can join your big ones.'

We ran into the garden to see the tree Rosie had brought. And as I bent to touch the leaves I suddenly saw Lucy Leadley-Brown's face, white and scared like in the classroom. And I wished I'd asked her to come. But how could I? Poor Lucy. Poor Hopper.

'Come on,' yelled Natasha.

'A tree's a funny present,' said Daniella.

'I think it's beautiful,' said Hannah.

We danced round the tree, singing to it. We must have looked crazy. So? We *were* crazy.

Chapter Four

TEACHER: Why are you late, Jimmy?

JIMMY: I'm not late, Sir. The bell is early. This is the earliest I ever come late.

TEACHER: Don't be silly, Jimmy, why are you late?

JIMMY: It was late when I left home.

TEACHER: Why didn't you start out earlier?

JIMMY: It was too late to start out earlier.

We sat in our circle while Melanie rabbited on for ever as usual. On and on and on. We'd had all this guff last time. I didn't care by now whether it was her dad hitting her mum or her mum hitting her dad or them both hitting the boyfriend. Why didn't Percy tell her to belt up? Mrs Thomson (our teacher) would've, but she was off on a course and Percy was captain for the day, yes sir. Percy's great but he's too kind – he can't put a stop to things. If Melanie carried on much longer, Tiro'd explode. And who could blame him? Tiro has as many problems as the rest of the school put together and never tells, Gowie says. And who should know better than Gowie with his history – the Terrible Sad History of Gowie Corby?

'Kill them ALL,' mutters Tiro. 'Fat fools. Like HER.'

'Now, Tiro, settle down,' says Percy nervously.

My gran says they didn't have Circle Time in her day. We have it often – too often, when Melanie or Tim and Hugh get going. My dad's better than your dad and so on, says Hugh. Tim gives us the weekend achievements – y'know, I scored fifty goals, played five Nintendo games, won the races in the park and played the clarinet better than any kid ever did, his dad says. Naomi tells us all about her favourite TV soap. Melanie gives us her home life, the latest in the ongoing family saga of Melanie's mum and dad. The rest of us don't say a lot. Some of us haven't got dads anyway. Some haven't got mums. Sometimes we use tags. You know:

'I'm happy today because . . .'

or 'I'm sad today because . . .'

We work round the class. That's when I get going on the Terrible Sad History of Gowie Corby, and they sit as if stuck with superglue. They like it. Especially Tiro. He actually sits still. Sometimes the tales are true. Sometimes I make them up from Gran's tales – she's a whizzo storyteller, Romany tales round the campfire. But sometimes I hate myself when I do this, as I get carried away and go over the TOP and Mrs Thomson looks slitty-eyed and if Gowie ever found out I was talking about him – well, life wouldn't be worth living and our life at Black Cat Cottage would be ruined.

But something was needed now. Hopper was gobbling to himself. Tiro was yawning. Any minute now we'd get the mad-parrot cry.

'We've just time for one more,' Percy said. 'Now, who shall it be?'

And she came through the door.

Head Fred was right behind her, beaming.

'Lucy has come back to us. She wasn't well before but she's now recovered and says she's ready to join in all our activities. Splendid, Lucy.'

She was wearing our red. Not purple, that had gone. She had all our school gear and my boots on her feet and her long hair caught up in a red ribbon. There were two red spots of colour on her cheeks and her chin stuck out.

'Make a space in our circle,' said Percy.

Hopper and Naomi waved hands and shuffled sideways. Silence.

Tiro leaned forward.

'Hey, Red Riding Hood, sit by me and I'll eat you up like the Big Bad Wolf.' He smiled. A drama student we had last year chose him for the lead in our class play because of that smile. She left in tears two weeks later, saying she'd rather do anything than teach. Sir (Mr Merchant) took over the play and Matthew took the lead. Matthew's reliable. Matthew's not mad.

Lucy Leadley-Brown looked at Hopper and Tiro.

'Oh, no, you scare me,' she said to Tiro.

Percy explained, 'This is when we talk to each other and get to know all about ourselves. Melanie's just finished. Find a seat, Lucy, and maybe you'd like to tell us something about yourself.'

She looked round. I moved and smiled. Well, why not? Let's find out about this girl who hated cats – and us, as far as I could see.

She sat down beside me, the red spots on her cheeks flaming.

'Try I'm sad because . . . or I'm happy because . . .' put in Naomi. 'Come on, Lucy. Whichever you like.'

'It's easy,' said Lucy at last. 'I'm sad because I don't want to be here at this rotten school and I wish I was dead.'

'Welcome to the club,' laughed Tiro, and made his mad-parrot cry.

Head Fred halted in the doorway, bobbing up and down a bit, like he does.

'Oh, Lucy, child, you don't mean that. You can't mean what you say. Not a nice girl like you. This is a lovely school. A wonderful, happy school. Isn't it, children?'

'Yes, Sir,' we all chorused faithfully. At least most of us did. Tiro showed the whites of his eyes like a mad horse.

'You'll love it here, Lucy. Just you wait and see. Naomi will take care of you. She's a good girl, Naomi.'

Tiro's amazing eyelashes were sweeping up and down and he was mouthing, 'Lovely Naomi. She's so lovely. Luvverly, luvverly, luvverly. I've got a luvverly bunch of Naomi-nuts.' I had to look the other way so as not to giggle. Then Lucy turned and spoke directly to me.

'Wait. I want to get something out of my bag.'

She went over to her bag, which was standing by Percy's desk – the purple bag. She fished something out of it: a small wallet. We watched as if hypnotized as she carried it back to the circle. What was she going to do? This was a good Circle Time. Better than *Grange Hill* or *Neighbours* even.

She sat down and opened the wallet. It had photographs in it. She looked through them as we waited, breathless. This new girl held us captive as Melanie never could. She finally selected a photograph and showed it to Percy, who looked at it then passed it on. Head Fred came and stood behind the circle and peered at it as well. When it came to my turn, I saw it was a snap of Lucy herself climbing out of a swimming pool laughing, long hair plastered to her head. Another girl floated in the water and another sat on the side, licking an ice-cream, with a golden retriever watching, panting, mouth open. Behind the girls loomed a large grey house covered with roses. It looked like Tara out of *Gone With the Wind* – you know, that old film about the Deep South in America, with Scarlett O'Hara in it. Come to think of it, Lucy L-B looked a bit like her. That sort of a girl.

'That was my home,' said Lucy. 'My dog. My friends. They're all gone now.'

Hopper held on to the photo for so long it had to be taken off him.

'You live in annuver country?' he gobbled at her.

She looked bewildered.

'He thinks you live in another country,' I explained.

'Why should he think that?'

'You should see where Hopper lives, that's why. It is another country.'

33

'Oh.'

'Tell us about it, Lucy,' said Head Fred. Then, micro-skirted Ms Bellis looked round the door – at least her top half did. The legs stayed behind the door. Head Fred waved her away. He also wanted to hear Lucy's story.

'What happened?' asked Percy.

Long pause as she waited, then she spoke at last: 'The only bad thing that's ever happened to me up till this summer was when that dreadful cat in the next house to us killed Peaches and it all began.'

Tiro jerked in surprise, and it takes a lot to surprise Tiro.

'Peaches? Peaches?'

'My hamster. Called Peaches.'

'I'm gobsmacked,' said Tiro, falling flat down on his back. 'Peaches!'

'And he came and laid Peaches at my feet. He didn't want to eat it . . .'

'No, they don't. Not hamsters. Must taste funny or something,' Naomi put in. 'I had this hamster once . . .'

'Didn't want to eat the peaches,' cried Hopper. 'I like peaches.'

'I cried for days. It was the worst thing ever. Till now.'

'What about now?'

'Couldn't be worse than a cat eating Peaches,'

Tiro put in, sitting up again. 'Nothing could.'

'Then everything happened. Then everything went wrong . . . And I'm here.'

Naomi rushed out of her place to embrace her but she shrank away. Hopper gobbled comfort but she buried her face in her knees and her hair fell all around. Into the silence the buzzer went and micro-skirt appeared in the doorway once more.

'You really must come, Sir. The chair of the governors is here.'

'On all four legs,' said Tiro. 'And speaking of legs . . .' He lay down full-length and gazed at Ms Bellis.

'I *suppose* the chair of the governors is more important than a desperately unhappy child,' I heard Head Fred mutter as he went out.

Mrs Thomson stood in the doorway, smiling, tall, bright hair, turquoise earrings with her turquoise sweater.

'Hello, Mr Percival. Hello, children. I'm back early. I'm pleased. It wasn't very good. Let's get the Maths equipment ready and then go and get a breath of fresh air. You all look as if you need it. So this is Lucy. We're very pleased to have you here. You'll get used to us. Come with me and I'll get you all your folders and equipment. Above all, don't worry, Lucy. We'll

35

sort things out. Zowey, check that the computer disks are in the right order and get things organized.'

Mrs Thomson's like a cool breeze blowing through the heat of our classroom. Everybody immediately looked normal, or as normal as a class could look that included Hopper and Tiro, and a beautiful girl weeping as if she would never stop.

Chapter Five

'Here's the mystery book you wanted.'
'But it's a Maths book!'
'Well, Maths was always a mystery to me.'

A low, steady noise – Mrs Thomson walking
from one group to another – everyone working,
and no one messing about, not even Tiro, glued
to a computer screen as always,* or Hopper using
a trundle wheel. We're on a conservation survey.
I was measuring with the roamer. One of the
groups was compiling a traffic-survey graph.

All was peace. Lucy was tucked up with
Naomi at a computer and I'd forgotten about
her until a loud, angry sob broke the peace and

* Tiro's a fantastic computer whizz kid, which is great when
every now and then he overdoes it and gets very withdrawn and goes quiet. He goes into the Internet, Cyber-
space. His dad's a computer freak, you see, and they've got
this set-up at his home. Sometimes he'll be withdrawn for
ages, and then it's peaceful at school and the teachers
worry about *him*. Then he comes down to earth, and to us,
and he's dreadful at school and we worry about *us*, 'cos
there's trouble all round.

hush. There she was, standing beside the computer and pointing at a small piece of paper pinned to the corner of the conservation murals and charts.

It said, 'Keep Cricklepit a quiet place to work. Shoot a seagull!'

'And next to it, 'Keep Cricklepit tidy. Eat a pigeon!'

'W. Merchant Rules, OK.'

Naomi was patting Lucy, who was trying not to be patted by Naomi, as anyone would.

Mrs Thomson moved across and asked her what was wrong.

'That,' cried Lucy. 'You're all horrible here. How can you have something like that on the wall?'

'But it's only a joke, Lucy. Mr Merchant likes jokes, so when he came and admired our work he left one for us.'

'He must be HORRIBLE!'

'No, he isn't. He's very kind and a keen conservationist, but he doesn't think people should take themselves too seriously.'

You could see this meant zilch to Lucy.

'Besides, I can't use the computer,' she went on. 'I've never had to use one before. And I don't understand any of this. They said I'd be much cleverer than the children here and I can't do any of it at all.'

'That's 'cos you're a moron,' shouted Tiro, and made his mad-parrot cry.*

'Get on with your work, children. No, Hopper, Lucy doesn't need your help. You go on with what you were doing. Tiro! Get on with yours too. Lucy and I are going to have a little chat. Come, my dear. The rest of you continue with what you're doing.'

I wanted to hear this little chat, but there was no way Mrs Thomson was going to let us in on that particular scene. After a while they emerged from the quiet corner. Lucy had stopped crying, but her face was set like an ivory mask. Mrs Thomson looked round at all of us and fixed on me at last.

'Zowey, you take Lucy and show her round the school and talk to her. Zowey likes a chat.' She grinned, but Lucy didn't. Off we went.

'Lucky Zowey, as usual,' I heard Tiro mutter. 'Should've been me.'

'Nobody would let you loose on a guided tour,' I hissed at him.

So, I showed her the hall, the grotty cloak-rooms and bogs, the new extension for the Infants, the PE apparatus, the wild garden we've made with the pond, the adventure play-ground, the libraries, the resource centre, the

*Then stopped as Mrs Thomson glared at him.

models and murals – the lot, everything I could think of. Last of all, I pointed out the school bell high above in its tower, the bell that was only rung once since the war, by a kid called Tyke Tiler, who fell off it, nearly got killed and almost wrecked the school. I talked like crazy, until at last we stopped and sat on a bench in the playground and looked at the tall old tree growing there.

'It's nearly a hundred years old,' I said. 'The school is even older. It was started in, oh, I forget, but something like 1660, and it was bombed in the war, but not the bell tower. And when there was a cholera epidemic they turned it into a hospital. This school has a great history. The vicar who wrote "Onward, Christian Soldiers" used to come and talk to the kids. The football team became our city football team. In the league, even if it isn't in the Premier League, you know,' I said, looking at her blank face.

At last *she* spoke. I'd been doing all the talking up till then.

'Who told you all that stuff?' she said slowly.

'Mr Merchant. Taught us last year. The joke person. He knows all about this school. It's a good school, he says.'

'What bilge! I never heard such rubbish. It's cheap and nasty and horrible and full of crooks

and boys like that gobbly creature! I hate it. I
hate it! I HATE IT!'

She went to run away, but I pulled her back.

'Look, what ideas have you got about us?
Somebody's been feeding you rubbish.'

'Candia told me about this school.'

Hadn't I heard that name before?

'Who the heck's Candia when she's home?
Sounds like a brand of toothpaste.'

'She's my friend. At least, she was.' The tears
started to flow again. 'But I don't think she'll
speak to me any more now.'

'Not much of a friend, then. Tell me more
about this Can-Can.'

'She's wonderful. She's clever and she's got
her own pony and she's very, very, very rich
and she'll go to the best boarding school in the
country and then to finishing school . . .'

'I hope they finish her off when she gets
there . . . What did she actually say?'

'When I told her that I'd got to leave Whiteoaks Grange and come here, she said . . .'

'Oh, look, stop crying, you wimp. Tell me
what Can-Can said and I can sort it out.'

'She said she wouldn't see me any more and
that you – you were all on drugs, on crack . . .
spoke horribly and bullied people who were
different . . . an' . . . an' you'd shove my head
down the dirty toilets!'

'You mean you've been crying over that . . . I don't believe it. Do you really think that?'

'I – I – don't know. But I'm scared.'

I wanted to shake her. I was suddenly angry with her, so angry I hissed like a snake.

'It's all much worse, Lucy Deadly-Brown. We torture kids regularly, Hopper's a cannibal and Tiro carries a knife for sticking into kids he doesn't like – stuck-up stupids like you!'

And at that moment Hannah appeared.

'Mrs Thomson says to bring Lucy in now, Zowey.'

'You take her in. I can't stand her,' I shouted, and rushed into school, slamming the door behind me. It was the first time I'd lost my temper in yonks. Me, wot never gets mad. The happy girl.

Chapter Six

'Be it ever so humble,
There's no-o-o-oo place like H-O-M-E!'

I'd managed to persuade Gran to help me with
my Maths homework as she's brilliant with
Maths and it was very tricky. Gowie was outside in the drive that runs from the *other* gate –
not the one with ROTTWEILERS on it. We've got
two, quite far apart. Very useful for Gowie
when he wants to get away from his girlfriends.
He's got dozens. He's bought an old banger of
a Jag, and spends every spare minute mending
and polishing and talking to it.

'Wonder you don't put it in nappies and give
it a bottle,' says my gran, but he takes no
notice. Just goes on tinkering and polishing.

When we'd finally finished the Maths and I
made yet another cup of tea, Gran said, 'That
girl you talked about has moved in down the
lane with *her* gran.'

'Oh, her.'

'Rupert did the removal. He doesn't charge

much. Said they couldn't afford one of the big firms. The old lady's a pain, he said, treated him like dirt. So he accidentally dropped a pink china shepherdess. On purpose.'

'Was she angry?'

'Very. But you know what Rupert's like. He's fine if you treat him nicely. Look out if you don't. Anyway, they'll be in a rare old muddle. Nobody's helping them. So you can take a Thermos and some sandwiches and say hello to the girl.'

'No, I won't.'

'Why not?'

'Mrs Thomson made me apologize to her for being rude. She hates us. For nothing. She's horrible to poor old Hopper, who thinks she's a fairy princess or something. And she's so WET. She cries all the time. She even pushes Hannah away. And Hannah is nicer than anybody. She'll never fit in with us lot.'

'You're still going over with tea and sandwiches. Number 14. The sandwiches are cut ready. Mabel did them. Very nice too. Special ones for grand ladies.'

Mabel is one of Gran's slaves. She turns up every day to run round after her and worship at the shrine. There's this idea that Gran mustn't get overtired, although she ran in the Marathon last year and was in the finals of the *Times*

Crossword Competition. She'd like to take up flying, she says.

'I'm not going to see that girl. She's a pain in the neck.'

'It's all ready in the kitchen. You needn't stay long. Go the back way. It's nearer.'

'No, I won't.'

But I did, of course. You can't argue with *her*.

So, there I was at Number 14, talking to the old lady, who was still unpacking.

'Thank you, child. Look at what those dreadful removal men did to my china shepherdess! Wicked! Workmen have no sense these days. They aren't prepared to do their jobs properly. What did you say your name was? Zoe? Foreign, are you? You look foreign, with those black curls and dark eyes.'

She made it sound as if it wasn't quaite naice to have black curls and dark eyes.

'I've got gypsy blood. Through my grandmother.'

'Oh. How extraordinary. Still, I suppose one can't be fussy.'

'No. Shall I pour you some tea? Gypsies make very good tea.'

She looked at me, her nose getting longer.

'Oh. Thank her for the tea. A gypsy, you say.'

'Well, my great-grandmother actually. I'm a throwback. You needn't worry. It's not catching.'

'Oh, I didn't mean that, child. No need to be touchy. You can't help it if there's gypsy blood. It was kind of your grandmother to send something. Nobody else has bothered to do anything for us. And as for the removal men – well!'

'Rupert's OK if you're nice to him and give him a good tip.'

The long nose quivered.

'You're a funny girl.' Then, 'Are you in Lucy's class?'

'Yes.'

'Well, go and talk to her. She won't eat. She just sits up there moping. Cries all the time.'

'She does that at school.'

'Talk to her. Please. Please.'

I'd have gone away if she hadn't said that second please, but . . .

'Where is she?' I asked.

'At the top. The attic. It'll be pretty when we've finished, but she can't see that.'

'OK. I'll go up. I'll take her a sarni. And I've got some chocolate.'

We sat like two bookends on the battered, flaking window-seat of Number 14, Black Cat Lane. There were no curtains. The windowpanes were grimy. On the bare boards stood a bed, a chair, a chest and a bookcase. There wasn't room for anything else.

Lucy sat, head on knees, hair everywhere, tangled and unwashed. She hadn't spoken to me. She pushed away the food I took up to her.

I sat. I didn't know what to say. I didn't like her and I'm not Naomi and I didn't want to give her advice and be full of caring whatnot and try to comfort her. It seemed to me, whatever black hole she was in she'd come out when she was ready and there wasn't much I could do. Till she stopped sorrowing for that old life, whatever it was, and got on with the new one here in Black Cat Lane and at Cricklepit School, she'd be a no-hoper, a pain in the neck. Rosie says I'm HARD.

So I waited. I looked through the grimy windows. Then I rubbed the nearest pane with a bit of paper hanky (shouldn't use those, Rosie says – think of the trees and the rain forests). I rubbed a bit more. The attic window was high and I could see the roofs and the church and the school bell tower and the tall tree in the playground. I could see the railway line and its steep embankment with the Wild Patch near Black Cat tunnel. I looked for Black Cat Cottage, but it was hidden by the trees.

Something moved – somebody, some people

– two figures scrambling down the embankment, half hidden by the bushes and dropping
on their bums down to the railway lines and
into the tunnel. I stood up and rubbed the
panes furiously. I tried to push open the
window but it was stuck. The figures looked
familiar. I knew them. I'd seen them on the
embankment before. Hopper – unmistakable,
like a giant toad following Tiro, who was
moving like a hunter towards the tunnel. Tiro
always led Hopper on. What were they doing?
They went into the tunnel. I watched its darkness, hypnotized. And then they came out and
Tiro ran to something by the side of the lines –
a heap of big stones. They must have collected
them earlier.

And I knew what they were going to do.
Gowie had told me how some boys long ago
had piled stones on the lines and a train had
nearly been wrecked. Tiro and Hopper were
going to do just that inside the tunnel . . .

'Come on. Come on. NOW!' I yelled. I
grabbed the sulking Lucy and hauled her after
me. She spoke. At last. She actually spoke.

'What is it? What are you doing? Are you
mad?'

'Shut up. Come on.'

I pulled her down the stairs, past the aston-
ished Grandma and out of the front door.

Down the lane I ran like a bat out of hell, like a
dog after a cat, pulling Lucy after me. I don't
know why, only she had to come too – come
on, come on, girl.

'Tell me . . .'

'Tiro – Hopper – lines – stones – accident!'

'What's-that-got-to-do-with-me? Huh, huh?'
she panted.

'People might get killed. Come on.'

We ran on. I knew I could get down to the
railway from our garden, though the bank was
very steep there. But that didn't matter. We'd
got to get those stones off the line. Think of
people who could be killed. It didn't bear thinking of. I wouldn't let them be killed. Lucy was
running as fast as me now, though I don't think
she knew what was happening. But I knew –
Danger Time and Zowey the Brave! Zowey to
the Rescue! Zowey Tops for Courage! Zowey
Corby Wins Children's Victoria Cross! Child of
the Year Award! Zowey Corby HEROINE!!!!

Under the laurel bush, over the fence, over
the barbed wire, sliding, bumping, half-falling,
panting, shrieking, we got there, splat, at the
bottom of the Wild Patch cliff. I'd dropped
Lucy's hand ages ago. You needed every hand
you'd got for grabbing plants, bushes, the
ground. I'd got a stitch, but it didn't stop me.
Move. Move.

And Lucy was running with me. Somehow she was pulling ahead, speeding as if she was getting away from everything. She might be a drip but she wasn't a wimp.

On to the railway lines. Under the dark tunnel.

'Look out for the trains.' I said.

'The tunnel's black. It's dangerous!'

'I know, I know. Just shift these stones, will you, kiddo.'

They were more than stones, they were rocks. And very heavy. They weighed a ton.

'Where are those awful boys?'

'Gone by now.'

I shouted, 'Tiro, Tiro', but the tunnel only re-echoed, Ti-ro, Ti-ro. Very eerie, very strange – making me feel afraid. We'd got all the stones off the rails, but not off the track. We pushed them to the side.

'Lucy, listen!'

'Is it a train?'

'Come on. Out of the way!'

'I'm scared.'

'Me, too.'

'Just this last big one . . .'

'Get the other end – NOW!'

'I can hear it coming . . .'

'Out of the tunnel. Quick! Quick! Run. NOW!'

We hurled ourselves, sweating, clutching, out
from under the tunnel and flung ourselves to
the side as the train chuffed safely through
Black Cat tunnel on the way to the station, not
fast, but fast enough to finish us.

We lay back on the embankment. Above us
in the evening sky a bird sang like an enchant-
ment. I looked at Lucy. Her hair was tangled
worse than the brambles. She'd got smuts on
her face and she was bleeding from scratches
everywhere.

But she wasn't crying!

She wasn't crying!

I nearly was. Now I'd stopped running I
ached all over, torn to bits; my new T-shirt was
ripped right off the shoulder.

Slowly we stood up and then . . .

'We did it.'

'We did it.'

'Yaaoooohow,' I yelled to the tunnel, the
embankment, everything! 'We're flaming
HEROINES, though no one'll believe it,' I sang
to the sky.

'Those boys – those boys have got away with
it. I hate boys,' cried Lucy. 'They ought to go to
prison . . .'

Someone else was yelling besides us. Someone dropped down the embankment, clearing
the brambles on six-foot legs. Someone was

calling us all the names you can think of, shouting and shaking his fists. Someone was using words Lucy could never have heard before.

'You stupid gits. You cretins. Didn't you see that train? What you doing down here? I'll lambast the living daylights out of you, Zowey Corby, so help me. I'll wring your blithering, stupid, half-witted neck. You know you're never supposed to come down here. You promised. Don't you know what happens to kids who mess about on railway lines? Don't you know anything? And who's this mindless, bone-witted moron you've got with you? Another of your rotten mates, I suppose. Just you two come back with me. You're going to Gran, you are . . . NOW MOVE!'

'Let me explain. It's not like you think. Listen. Listen!'

'No, you listen to me. No, I won't tell Gran, because she'd worry and it's not worth upsetting her for two half-wits like you . . . whoever *you* are!'

'Listen to me. Please, please, PLEASE LISTEN,' I shouted.

Lucy whispered, 'Please listen.'

He took another look at her and simmered down slowly.

'Right. But it'd better be good, Zowey.'

'Tiro and Hopper put rocks on the line. I saw

them. They ran off. But we – we – saved the train.' I said my bit and burst into tears. TO MY HORROR AND SHAME.

Lucy spoke quietly. 'That's true. I swear it. Zowey was super. She made me come. She made me help clear the line. She saved the train. Just like the story.'

'Which way did that pair of villains go?'

'Through the tunnel,' Lucy said.

'Right, I'm after them. They'll wish they'd never been born. Get home, you two. Quit bawling, Zowey. I only shouted a bit. Right, I'm gone.'

And he was.

'Who was that?' Lucy asked at last as we crawled back up the cliff and past the Wild Patch.

'My brother, Gowie,' I sniffed.

She paused, hanging on to a bit of bush.

'Isn't he wonderful?' she panted. 'I've never met anybody like him.' Her eyes shone. Her cheeks were pink. Could this be Weepy Lucy?

I was too out of breath to reply. I felt terrible. And anyway, all I needed was another addition to the fan club. I'd heard it all before.

'There's a queue,' I panted, but she didn't hear.

Coming down the bank had been awful. Climbing back up was WORSE!

Chapter Seven

Dear Aunt Claire
   I feel like jumping off a cliff because
the zits on my face keep popping and my
friend has left me! What shall I do?
   Yours,
   Zitto Popper

Dear Zitto
   Jump.
   Yours,
   Aunt Claire

Gowie burst into the kitchen. 'Those little devils
got away,' he said.

We sat drinking tea with Gran. We'd show-
ered and put cream on our scratches and stings.
Lucy wore a clean T-shirt and jeans. Mine.
Blanket purred on her knee. She looked eagerly
at Gowie, eyes shining.

'Will they get punished? They *can't* get away
with it! My dad says . . .' She stopped, her face
suddenly pale.

'What does your dad say, then?' asked Gran after a minute.

She shook her head and wouldn't answer. The old look she'd worn in school settled back on her face.

Gowie said slowly, 'I shan't go to the police about them because they're already in trouble.'

'But they ought to be *severely* punish – ' She stopped again.

'My dear, nearly everyone needs to be severely punished about something,' Gran put in, 'Gowie most of all.'

'Don't be unfair. I've reformed! But I'll get that pair. Don't tell people about it, though. I'll deal with it.'

'Not Rosie,' I said. 'She doesn't need to be punished. She's good all through.'

And as if she'd heard, there came a knock on the door and there she was.

'Hello, who are you?' She smiled at Lucy.

'Lucy. She's a friend of Zowey's,' replied Gran.

I waited for her to say she wasn't, but she managed to smile, just. I hoped she wouldn't start flipping crying and bawling again.

'Yeah. Mm. Lovely, isn't she?' Gowie grinned, oozing fatal charm all over the room. 'I'll save her for later.' And he smiled to show her he didn't mean it.

It was enough to make you throw up but

she turned pink and sort of dimpled. Yuck.

'You're enough to make anyone sick,' I pointed out. 'You're so VAIN AND CONCEITED.'

'But he won't be for long,' Rosie added. 'Heather, Ruth and Lorraine are heading in this direction. Apparently you've promised to take them all out . . .'

'Well?'

'At the same time. On the same evening. You never did have any memory.'

'Oh, no! They're not coming here?'

'Mm. Oh, yes, they are. They're pretty mad at you as well.'

'And actually – ' Rosie paused – 'you *almost* promised me you'd come with me to that meeting about solving the motorcar problem.'

'Oh, I'm sorry, Rosie, but it's not my scene, really.'

'Oh, Gowie!'

'I'm sorry, Rosie. Truly. Oh, Lord, is that them?' as voices were heard approaching up the drive. 'I love you, Rosie. Bye. See you.'

He disappeared and I heard the French windows banging as he rushed away, Lucy staring after him.

'That's why we have two entrances a fair way apart,' explained Gran, pouring out more tea. 'It's to let Gowie have lots of exits.'

*

'What I've really come for,' Rosie said to Gran as she settled into a chair and a cup of tea, 'is this.'

She fished two leaflets out of her bag. I peered across at them.

One leaflet read:

OPT OUT!
ENSURE THE BEST OF ALL POSSIBLE FUTURES
FOR CRICKLEPIT SCHOOL!

The other said:

CAMPAIGN FOR PARENTS AGAINST
OPTING OUT!
DON'T WRECK THE SYSTEM!
THERE IS NO GOING BACK FOR CRICKLEPIT
SCHOOL!

Ever since I've known Rosie Lee (which is as long ago as I can remember), she has been trying to make the world a better place, especially for children. Sometimes she almost gives up and I once saw her cry – over Gowie, of course – but she always bounces back. And she was bouncing now, hair shining, teeth gleaming, hair spiralling.

'You'll come on the committee with me, won't you, Lilian – ' that's my Gran – 'please. We need your common sense and organ-ization!'

'Hey! Don't let's get carried away. What's it all about?'

'Half the teachers and governors at the school want to go it alone and be self-governing, the other half want to stay within the system. The parents have to vote on it.'

'I'll have another cup of tea and think about it,' said Gran. 'Come to think of it, a glass of whisky might help the brain cells.'

'Whisky kills brain cells,' put in Lucy.

'You're a boring child,' said Gran. 'Where did we get you? I can't kill my brain cells as I doubt if I ever had any in the first place!'

Lucy sat there gobsmacked, and I giggled inside. It was true. She *was* boring, though OK when she ran down the bank and pulled the stones off the line.

'You want me to help, do you?' asked Gran.

'I want *you* on the committee,' nodded Rosie. 'If our school opts out, all the rest will want to and it will just be grab, grab, grab and sucks to everyone else.'

'Why would you want to help that horrible place?' Lucy's face was red, angry, eyes wide, tears shining.

'Oh, don't start crying again!' I shouted. 'I thought you'd packed that in.'

Rosie Lee went on her knees beside Lucy, now hidden behind all the hair again.

'I'm not crying!' came a muffled voice
through the hair.

'Tell me about it, Lucy,' Rosie murmured.

'Some idiot called Candy-Floss or something
says we're all on drugs, stick heads down loos,
bully everybody and do no work. She had to
leave this *Gone With the Wind* place where they
all had swimming pools and ponies and ate
peaches, and slum it here with us . . .'

'I asked Lucy, not you, Zowey, thank you,'
said Rosie. 'You tell me what's wrong, Lucy.'

'Well, it's not really like what she says. But I
can't tell you. I can't tell anyone how I feel. I'd
better go. My grandma will be worrying. Thank
you for the tea,' she said to mine.

'That's all right. Any time you feel like having
a good weep and giving me a talk on the evils
of drink, I'll be here with a cup of tea.'

'My grandma says I shouldn't cry and give
way.'

'Well, I think it's OK to have a good howl
and yell and get over it, whatever it is. Zowey,
see her home now. Oh, and tell *your* grandmother she's welcome to come in for a cup of
coffee.'

Talking, I led her through to the garden:
'OK. Sorry, Lucy, you can yell if you want to.
And I know Tiro and Hopper are enough to
drive you potty, but there are some nice ones,

59

esp Hannah and Sue Wong, and Daniella, though she's a bit showy-off. We're the Cool Cricklepit Cats, our crowd, our lot.'

As we went through the hall, I picked up my flute, which I hadn't packed away, and tootled a bit. I couldn't help it, it was so beautiful. She stopped.

'But . . . but . . . you're good. That's really something.'

'Do you play?'

'Only the recorder.'

'Oh, come and join the orchestra. It's terrific. We're doing *The Jungle Book* for the school musical at the end of term. It'll be great. And stop crying and be one of our Cricklepit Cats. Come on, Lucy. Don't let the —* get you down, as Gowie says.'

She'd got her wide stare again. I think she was shocked.

'I dunno.'

'OK. Suit y'self. Here, get quickly through the laurel bush and there's your house, Number 14.'

She squeezed through, followed by Ratbag, gave a very little wave and was gone.

Rosie and Gran were still yacking when I got

*I'm not allowed to write down this word: censored.

back. Rosie looked up to say, 'That's an unhappy girl there. Be nice to her, Zowey.'

'She's such a silly snob. Goes on all the time about her other school . . .'

'Which one was it?'

'Whiteoaks Grange. You know, up at the top of the hill.'

'Oh, that one. Yes, I know it. All girls. Exclusive. Expensive.'

'Purple,' I said. 'Is it that good?'

'It's all show. No resources and underpaid teachers. But they talk nicely. No swearing, Zowie!'

I tootled my flute at her and then went up to bed before I got roped in to deliver leaflets and address envelopes. After a bit I got to thinking about all the mixed-up kids, and what would happen to Tiro, Hopper and Lucy. When I'd finished with them, there was the school trip and beginning to get ready to do the school musical. Plenty going on, plenty, plenty. At last I sat in bed listening to my Walkman and thought of us in Black Cat Cottage, trees all round, railway line just below and the river even further below, going out to sea. Outside all sorts of horrible things could be happening, I thought. But here I was. Maybe danger wasn't such a good thing. Maybe here with a book, a Walkman and my flute was better. Fat Blanket crept through the door and sat asking to be lifted on to the bed. Lazy fleabag! But I snuggled him in with me all the same.

Chapter Eight

'We're going to the zoo – zoo – zoo!
What about you?
You can come too!'

As we set off in the coach Tiro took a toilet roll
out of Mrs Thomson's first-aid bucket and
threw it through the window. The strong wind
blowing took it and threw it in the air, so that it
unwrapped the twirling pink paper round and
round the school railings and ended up trailing
over the cars and the bottom branches of the
big tree in the playground, just like in the
puppy ads.

'Get that sorted out QUICKLY,' roared Mr
Merchant, who was coming with us. And Tiro
hopped out to wind the paper up in a heap, an
angelic smile on his face.

'It looks very pretty,' said Sue Wong.

'So does Tiro,' giggled Daniella.

'Oh, stick to pop stars. They're safer,' I said.

The Cats were all crammed together in two
seats.

The boys had the long seat at the back, naturally.

'Quieten down. From the sound of it, we don't need to be going to the zoo. It's going with us,' Mr Merchant said. 'Mrs Thomson, shall we leave Tiro behind?'

'No, I don't think so. But he can sit by *me*.'

You should've seen Tiro's face.

'All right, then, you can sit by Hopper. But if you two mess about, that's the last outing this term for you!'

'I'll be good. Like an angel . . .'

'Reasonably well behaved will do, thanks.'

'Sir, I want to see the tiger, please,' Tiro said humbly.

'We all want to see the tiger,' loadsa voices called. And at last we were off, only five minutes late.

We were going to the zoo because we were about to start on our musical, *The Jungle Book*, and Mrs Merton – the music teacher, and Mr Merchant, who were running the whole thing, wanted us to have a dekko at some real animals before we actually started. We'd also got to read Kipling's *The Jungle Book*.

'Can't we just watch the film?' asked Melanie.

'You can read the book as well,' said Mrs Thomson. 'Without it there'd've been no film.'

'And take a good look at the animals, how they move, look at their eyes . . .'

'I don't like to look at the eyes,' said Sue. 'That's because their eyes are sad.'

'That's because they're in a zoo,' said Hannah.

'I don't know what to think about zoos,' I said.

None of us did, but now we were on our way in the coach we were looking forward to seeing them, although we didn't like the idea of zoos. Anyway, it was great to be out wearing casual clothes, carrying packed lunches and off for the day with friends.

The coach bristled with Walkmans, bags of sweets and crisps, and long coloured bags like Smartie packets.

'No eating sweets until you've had your packed lunches,' announced Percy, standing up at the front. All the sweets disappeared. Jaws chewed gum instead.

Roland, a tiny grasshopper boy with yellow hair and a sharp nose, was pushed down between the seats while the boys all piled their bags on him more and more and more.

'Leave him,' Lucy cried. 'He'll suffocate. Get them off him, Mrs Thomson. That boy will suffocate.'

'He'll be all right,' I shouted to her. 'Wait and see.'

Sure enough, two seconds later there came a mad shriek from where she sat with Naomi and Melanie, as Roland popped up in the middle of them like a Jack-in-a-Box.

'Oh! Oh! Take him away,' she screamed, and shrieks of laughter hit the air.

Mr Merchant surveyed us all. 'School trips are the nearest thing to hell that any teacher can imagine. Just quieten down or we shall turn the coach round and go back for spelling tests.'

At that moment Tiro attempted to balance on the edge of a seat.

'That's it,' said Sir. 'You sit by me. Move over, Hopper.'

'I haven't got to sit by Hopper, have I?' said Percy, moving reluctantly. 'Oh, dear!'

'This hurts me more than it does you,' said Mr Merchant, as he sat by Tiro.

'I haven't reached my sell-by date yet. Unlike you, Sir,' answered Tiro.

'One more word and I'll put you off the coach, here in the middle of nowhere.'

'The European Commission'll do you for it, Sir.'

'It would be well worth it,' replied Mr Merchant.

'I've never been anywhere with boys before,' I heard Lucy say. 'It's horrible.'

But she was grinning and looked quite cheerful for once.

And so we arrived. I'm not gonna tell you about it because you've all been on school visits and this isn't a school-visit story. But we decided that zoos might be OK after all when our guide had explained to us about the work they were doing for conservation and that some species would have died out without this. Besides, the zoo covered a gynormous area – we were knackered by the time we'd walked everywhere, seen everything and eaten our packed lunches. Percy got lost and so did two boys from another class, but then somebody always gets lost, and Tiro threw Roland's shoes in the lake – though, as Mrs Thomson pointed out, they should have been on Roland's feet.

But it was a fantastic trip and we drew pictures and made notes on our clipboards. It had been a good day.

'I think I quite like zoos after all. The animals all look wonderful,' Lucy said in her carrying voice, as a bunch of us made our way back to the bus.

'But that one doesn't,' said a voice, and we watched the tiger on the hill slope – the handsomest creature there.

So powerful –

So beautiful —

He paced backwards and forwards against his high fence on his wooded hillside. He had lots of room but we knew he was in prison. Back and forwards he paced, forwards and back, back and forwards.

In the next enclosure the lions – a whole pride of them hung in trees or slept or groomed one another, completely laid-back. Different, very different.

But not the tiger. His hillside was large, the sky was blue, but . . .

'He's in prison,' cried Hopper's gobbly voice. 'I'm gonna let him out.'

And he ran to the padlocked gate.

'Don't be stupid,' snapped Tiro, grabbing him, and, twisting his arm behind his back, marched him along with us.

'Oh, do leave Hopper alone,' Mrs Thomson called out as we went along. 'He's not doing any-thing. And let's hurry. We're running a bit late.'

As we got on the coach with Hopper sobbing and saying he must set the tiger free over and over again, she asked, 'Did you enjoy that outing, Zowey? Has it changed your mind about zoos?'

'Well, I liked it and I thought most of the animals were fine . . . But,' I said, 'I don't know about the tiger.'

'He's like Tiro,' Hannah added. 'Unhappy.'

'And that,' said Sue, 'makes them dangerous. Like Tiro. We're all scared of Tiro, just as we're all scared of tigers.'

Chapter Nine

TIRO TO HOPPER (who was helpfully clean-
   ing up the mess he'd made in Art
   lesson): 'I see you've joined the other
   side now.'

'I'll look after you,' gobbled Hopper to Lucy.
   'I can look after myself, thank you very
much. Go away. No! Don't you dare touch me!'
   Hopper sniffed sadly. He loved Lucy madly,
truly, desperately (and all the rest). He'd never
loved anyone before, except for a week when
he'd trailed round after me. But Lucy was his
princess, his vision that the world might be a
different place from the one he'd always lived
in, mumbling and gobbling, being told to get
lost, push off, belt up, cretin, idiot, spastic.
Lucy also told him to get lost, but coming from
her it was different.
   Lucy walked away from Hopper and joined
Naomi and Melanie under the tree in the play-
ground. She hadn't taken up my offer to join
us, the Cricklepit Cats.

'Why does she go around with those two?' I wondered.

'I think they make her feel secure,' said my gran to me when I told her.

'Whatja mean? Those two are yuck.'

'Oh, it gives her confidence to feel superior to the kids at your place. Don't you see, she's got to be better, or all she's grown up with is lost as well as her home, parents, dog and pony?'

'I can't follow all that. I'd've thought she'd have liked Hannah!'

'Look, how could she feel superior to Hannah? And even Daniella is richer and more with-it than her friends at Whiteoaks Grange, yet she's here at this school that Lucy thinks is so terrible.'

'Oh, you're too clever for me. I just want to be happy and enjoy myself. And everyone else the same.'

'So do we all,' said Gran. 'So do we all.'

Hopper brought a messily wrapped little package for Lucy.

'I brought you a prezzie,' he gobbled, face purple and full of hope.

'I don't want it. Take it away.'

Lucy's nose stuck in the air and she looked like her grandmother. Hopper pushed the parcel at her.

'He's just stupid. People like him ought to be put down,' Naomi said.

'I didn't know there were any people like Hopper before I came here,' Lucy added, and, holding the parcel at arm's length, she sashayed across the classroom and dropped it in the waste bin, watched by her admiring fan club, Naomi and Melanie. Hopper stomped away to a table in the corner and buried his head in his hands.

The mad-parrot cry came louder than usual as Tiro did a kind of leap and landed in front of Lucy, glaring wildly, his features somehow sliding off his face. I turned away, for I don't like to look into Tiro's eyes. Lucy stepped backwards to her seat.

'I know it's hard for you, but wouldn't you just like to be nice for once and say thank you?' he spat at her.

'There's – no – no – reason why I should have to t-take it because he-he wants to give it to me. I don't want him to give me things. I didn't ask him to!'

She'd got a point there, but Tiro wasn't taking it. He grabbed her arm and started to pull her towards the bin. They were the same height, but Tiro was stronger and he pushed her arm down into the bin.

'Now just you pick up Hopper's prezzie. You

don't know what he's done to get that for you.'

Hannah caught my eye. Just what had Hopper done to get whatever was in that rotten-looking package? Shoplifting? Mugging? Stealing off his mum? Robbing a little kid? Nicking from the cloakroom? Whatever it was, Tiro would be the brains and organization behind it. Tiro would be involved.

'Took 10p off his father, I suppose,' Lucy sneered, pulling back.

'Yes, what did he do, Tiro?' asked Matthew, for even the other boys were listening, the ordinary ones who play football and rugby and Nintendo and collect stamps and play chess and sing in the choir and go to Scouts and Woodcraft and athletics and get on with their lives just like the Cricklepit Cats get on with theirs.

'He asked his dad for some pocket money,' said Tiro slowly. One or two kids giggled. But not me. I know his dad. If you see Hopper's dad, head swiftly in the opposite direction, Gowie told me.

'Did he get the money?' asked Matthew (who I know a bit, and now and then go out with – secretly – and he's great, and I could tell he wished he'd never started asking about this, but would like to get on with whatever he was doing before).

'Yeh,' answered Tiro. 'And when his dad finished beating him black and blue, he gave him some money. And guess what Hopper did with it?'

'What?' asked Melanie.

'He spent it *all* – more money than he'd had *all year* – on buying a present for Miss Deadly-Bum here!'

Lucy flushed scarlet.

'I'm going to fetch Mrs Thomson,' squealed Naomi.

'Don't . . . anyone . . . move!' yelled Tiro.

Gobsmacked, we stood. Frozen. And then, then, I cried, 'TIRO! Stop it! Don't look like that. It isn't worth it. It's all right. Lucy, take that parcel. Now! Say thank you to Hopper. He's only human. He won't hurt you, though Tiro might. Quick! Before Mrs Thomson comes in!'

The Cricklepit Cats had moved up all around me and we now stood together confronting Lucy, Hopper and Tiro.

Lucy picked the grubby little package out of the bin. Hopper lifted up his tear-stained face.

'Thank you,' said Lucy.

'Thank you, Hopper,' said Tiro.

'Thank you, Hopper,' she said.

'Open it. Please!' Hopper mumbled.

She stood there.

'Get on with it!' I yelled. 'Mrs Thomson'll be here any minute now!'

Lucy tugged at the twisted Sellotape, pulled off the dirty ribbon, the cheap wrapping paper, the grey cotton wool and stared and stared at what was in it.

'Oh,' she said. 'Oh, I didn't know. Hopper, I didn't know. Oh, Hopper.'

'But what was it?' asked Gran, over supper.

'A brooch. Blue and silver flowers. Enamel. Absolute magic. The prettiest brooch I ever saw. Lucy was just shattered.'

'Poor Hopper,' said Gran.

'I don't believe a word of it,' Gowie put in. 'Hopper's dad's never got any money. He's on Social Security and drinks the lot the minute he gets it.'

'Then where did Hopper get the money to buy that beautiful brooch?'

'Don't ask me. Ask Tiro. That brooch could have come from anywhere and probably did. Tell Lucy not to wear it till it's been checked.'

'Oh, that makes me sad,' I cried.

'Don't be. You know Tiro.'

'Yeah. But – but he is good to Hopper, y'know.'

'That's 'cos he thinks he owns him. Hopper's Tiro's slave. Or his pet monkey.'

'Gowie, how can you say such things?' cried Rosie from the doorway, just coming in.

'Because they're true. But what are you doing here, beautiful?'

'We're off to a meeting, remember? "To opt or not to opt" – that is the question. Come on.'

'Not me – I've got a date,' said Gowie disappearing.

'Then Zowey had better come with us, as there'll be no one in.'

'Yes, I'll come. I'll get my anorak.'

Chapter Ten

PERCY TO HOPPER: What do you want to do
  when you grow up?
HOPPER: I don't know. What do you want
  to do when you grow up?

The school hall was jam-packed full of parents,
kids, journalists, photographers. All the seats
were taken so Hannah, Natasha and me were
standing against the wall-bars. On the platform
were the Mayor (Natasha's dad!), Head Fred,
the school governors including Hannah's dad,
Professor Fox, and Rosie Lee, only one of three
women and the only one young and black. My
gran sat near the back doing her crossword
puzzle. She looked up and winked at me.
Gowie was nowhere to be seen, as he said it
wasn't his scene.

After a lot of rumbling, shuffling and milling
round, people settled down. Cameras flashed at
the platform.

Head Fred stood up to speak.

'I'm happy to welcome all of you, Mayor,

governors, parents and children, to this important meeting which affects the whole future of
the school. We are going to discuss whether
this school, Cricklepit Combined, should stay as
it is under the control of the Local Education
Authority or whether it should opt out and run
all its own affairs – in other words, go it alone. I
hope tonight's discussion will help us to decide
which way to go when the parents are asked to
vote at the end of this term. So it gives me great
pleasure to ask the Mayor to start the discussion rolling.'

People clapped politely as Natasha's dad
(wearing his chain) stood up on the platform.
After he'd greeted everyone there (except us)
he went on . . .

'If we opt for independent control we shall
get extra financial support from the government
and various interests in the town. We can have
new classrooms, extra playing fields, com-
puters, new equipment, a new theatre for our
children. Our children will have the best. Our
children will be the most successful in the
town. Our school will be a SUCCESS! Our
school will be TOP! So I beseech all of you,
"Let's opt out!" '

He sat down amid loud applause from the
front of the hall.

Hannah's father rose to his feet and Hannah

stared at him, her face pink. Hannah's dad was cool.

'This city has an excellent educational record. All the city's schools work well together. If our school opts out it will upset the balance, others will follow suit and there will be chaos. The promised money will undoubtedly run out and instead of golden eggs we shall be holding broken ones in our hands. Our children's future is at stake. Don't gamble. Vote for what you know works.'

He sat down to claps and cheers.

Other people got up and said all the same things over again, as if we hadn't heard them properly the first time. They droned on and on.

I blanked off a bit, yawning and wondering why things that are *important* and good can be boring. And I thought about something Mrs Thomson told us today – that some old Anglo-Saxon geezer said life was like a bird – a sparrow, I think – flying out of the dark, cold and wild night outside into a hall full of light and warmth and being there for a while and then flying out into the dark again. I shivered a moment and looked at the windows. For a while I thought I saw Tiro's face against the windowpane, frightening, eyes black pits, mouth open. I nudged Hannah, standing next to me, but when she looked he'd gone.

*

More speeches. Children started to shuffle their feet. People chattered. But Rosie Lee stood up like a thin black sword. Her voice rang out like a bell. The hall was silent.

'His Worship the Mayor brings temptations like the Devil showed to Christ in the wilderness. We shall have all the toys and we shall be top. Is that what education's about?

'I went to this school and I loved it and it taught me well. This school has cared for hundreds of children who stepped inside its sheltering walls – the successful, the greats – and there have been quite a few of those who have attended here, and I hope there will be many more in the future – but it also taught and cared for the others, the lonely, the lost and the damaged. Our school can go on doing its marvellous work without damaging the other schools like us in the city. For that is what may happen if we grab everything going like greedy children. No man is an island and, I tell you, no school is an island either. We are all part of society. We are all on this planet. We must do the best for us, yes, but not, not always at the expense of others.

'These goodies we are promised are not guaranteed. Already elsewhere promises are not being carried out and overblown projects are failing. This could happen to us too.

'Our school has been happy and successful in the past and can continue to do well in the future without opting out. So please, I ask you, vote against opting out!'

My hands hurt as I clapped and cheered. Half the audience were standing and shouting. Rosie Lee's teeth – you've got more teeth than a dental factory, Gowie used to say – flashed as she smiled at the hall, loving it all, you could tell, glad to be alive, to be on her feet speaking for what she believed in. Rosie Lee would stand up to the whole world for what she believed in, went through my head. She'd managed to get people going – in fact two men were going so much they were nearly scrapping as one shouted, 'I only care about *my* kid!' and the other, 'No, it's my kid deserves the best!'

But someone near the back got up and shouted, 'What's it got to do with you, you black cow? Get back to the trees!'

'Out! Out! Out!'

A scuffle at the back of the hall, people stood on their chairs, shouting, getting up and waving their hands.

'Opt out!'

'Don't opt out!'

'Opt out!'

'Don't opt out!'

Head Fred was bobbing, the governors trying to calm things.

And the swing doors opened and in shot Hopper, face streaky, anorak half off, one trainer missing, sliding, rolling, trying to grab a chair as he flew past.

Somewhere behind him sounded a mocking laugh and the wild, crazy cry of Tiro.

The meeting got going again. Hopper had been removed by Mrs Thomson and more people stood up to speak, until at last we all went out noisily, talking, arguing, into the night.

'What a good meeting,' I heard someone say. 'We aired a few viewpoints.'

'Come on,' said Gran, suddenly beside me. 'We're not hanging about in this.' She grabbed my arm and made her way through the play-ground like a little tank, her umbrella at the ready.

'Wait for me,' called Rosie Lee, who came up behind us and seized my other arm, and we made our way through the cars in the play-ground, under the great old tree swaying above us. The wind was getting up. The tree creaked; the sound was eerie. I shivered, for the night was cold.

Outside the school gates, behind the bushes, dark shadows waited.

'Here she comes,' one said. 'Black bossy cow.'

'No, monkey. Black bossy monkey.'

They moved in.

'Go home. Go back up the trees where you belong.'

'Black scumbag.'

'You get out of my way, silly old fool,' said one to Gran.

She hit him with her umbrella, then turned on the one who was hitting Rosie. But another one knocked Gran to the ground.

People walked past taking no notice. People we knew. I screamed and screamed and yelled.

A tall figure pushed among us.

'Take that, you ruffian! You utter scum!' bellowed a voice, upmarket, bossy, full of command. 'The police are on their way! You all ought to be locked up. Hooligans! Garbage!'

Right, left and centre, shouting at the top of her voice, Mrs Leadley-Brown laid about her with her walking stick. She was taller than they were and jumping with rage. Gran, half her size, struggled up and joined her, hitting out with her umbrella. And hit me. As I sank dazed to the ground, the National Front gang fled into the night.

We all dusted ourselves down and investigated our bruises. Rosie seemed OK. I felt wobbly.

'I think we'd all better come to my place,' said Gran, 'and have a cup of tea. Or something stronger, if you prefer. Oh, I ache.'

'So do I, me dear. So do I. A drop of brandy would be very acceptable.'

'Whisky,' said Gran. 'Whisky it shall be.'

'You coming as well?' I asked Lucy, who'd silently joined us. 'Fancy a Coke?'

'Yes, please.'

We set off with Rosie. All the world now turned up to offer help, including Sergeant Price and Head Fred, hurrying along after us, but the two grandmothers, one tall and one short, went on ahead down the road, talking nineteen to the dozen about the horrors of the world today and taking no notice of any of 'em.

But Gowie told Rosie later that she was an idiot to stick her neck out for what didn't actually concern her.

'You just want to look after yourself and the ones you care about,' he said. 'That's what it's all about. Otherwise you get hurt.'

'But I care about the whole world,' said Rosie Lee, 'even if I do get hurt.'

So they had a row, then ended up snogging. I know 'cos I saw 'em.

Chapter Eleven

'When is it unlucky to cross the path of a
  Black Cat?'
'When you are a mouse.'

After school the phone rang. I answered it, as
Gran and Gowie suffer from paralysis in the
legs when the phone rings.

'Is that Lilian Corby?' asked a female
voice.

'No, Zowey.'

'Would you fetch her for me, child?'

I covered the mouthpiece and hissed,
'Gran, it's for you. Mrs Leadley-Brown.'

We pulled faces at one another. What was all
this about, then?

'Yes, of course,' she said. 'I'll be there as fast
as I can.'

She put down the phone and pulled another
funny face at me.

'Come on. We're off to the supermarket.'

'What for?'

'She didn't say. But she sounded peculiar and

said would I come as quickly as possible. We're needed.'

'What for?' I said again.

'She didn't say. But she did sound, well, humble.'

'Don't be silly, Gran.'

'I know. I probably imagined it. Anyway, come on. I don't want to go on my own. And put something warm on. It's cold outside. Where are the car keys?'

'You won't need me.' Gowie spoke from the depths of an armchair. 'It's not far. I've got a lot of work to do. I'm way behind.'

'That doesn't surprise me . . .'

Gran was hunting irritably for the keys.

'. . . you've spent hours on that useless heap of machinery out there and you've been carrying on with one girl after another . . .'

'That's all changed. I'm a reformed character. I'm going to go out with just Rosie and no one else.'

' 'Cos she'll help you with your work!'

'No, she's always been the only one I care tuppence for. You must know that. And I'll sell the Jag.'

'I'll believe that when I see it. Ah, there they are. I knew I'd put them somewhere. Come on, Zowey. What are you hanging about for? We've got to hurry.'

'I've been ready for ages. Just waiting for you.'

I peered out of the car windows as we got stuck in a tailback, the street jam-packed, hooters blaring angrily, uselessly. I wondered who was out there in the dark night among the snarling cars and tired motorists, beasts on the prowl in the car jungle.

'Suppose we get mugged,' I said.

'Don't be silly. Anyway, you're in worse danger from pollution. And don't worry. I've brought pepper and an umbrella with me.'

'Pepper?'

'Yes. If anyone tries anything in the car-park, I'll send pepper up his nose and hit him with the umbrella. And if the police say pepper's an offensive weapon, I'll say I got it at the super-market. Ah, we're moving at last.'

'The trouble is it's Thursday and it'll be crowded,' she went on.

It was.

I could see loads of people I know. Some I waved to. And I tried *not* to see Hopper with his dad and I hoped they didn't see me.

Lucy waited with *her* grandma by the cash till. Mrs Leadley-Brown stuck out like a sore thumb in her smart suit (mauve tweed). *My* gran wore leggings and an old jacket. Lucy looked like she did on that first day at school, pale, with her chin stuck out and red spots on her cheeks. And as if she might break if you pushed her too hard.

'They won't accept any of my cards. They've taken them from me,' said the old lady. 'My cheque book as well, and I haven't enough cash to pay for the food in the trolley and we've none in the house. Can you help? Lilian? You're the only friend I could bear to ask.'

Lucy wasn't looking at me and I felt so sorry for them as they were proud people. Gran wouldn't have cared tuppence . . . just shouted a bit. But what sort of friends did they have if we were the only ones they could turn to?

Gran went up to the girl at the check-out, a big blonde girl straight out of a TV soap.

'I'll pay,' she said.

'Oh, it's you, Mrs Corby. 'Ow's Gowie keeping? 'Aven't seen 'im lately. 'E used to take me out sometimes, y'know.'

'Yes, Marilyn, I know.'

'Oh, 'e's wicked, 'e is. But you can't help liking 'im. Oh, you're going to pay, are you? Right. Then you'll just 'ave to wait a moment, Mrs C, for the manager.'

She turned to Mrs Leadley-Brown, waving her hand in the air. 'Don't you mind, m'dear. 'Appens all the time. Why, only last week a

coach company wasn't paid – the cash hadn't
come through – and lots of 'em had their cards
stopped, poor things. Terrible, init? On your
pension, are you? Ah, well, we're all 'ard up
these days. But we must keep smiling, mustn't
we?'

Lucy wasn't smiling. She looked as if she
wanted to die there and then.

'Marilyn,' said Gran. 'I shan't keep smiling if
the manager doesn't come soon.'

'Oh, 'e won't be long.'

Marilyn's wide smile took in Mrs Leadley-
Brown, all the poor and anyone who couldn't
pay for the food in their trolleys.

I tugged at Lucy's sleeve.

'Let's wait outside,' I said.

'Oh, yes.' She was near to tears.

We started to make our way to the exit and at
that moment Hopper spotted us.

It was cold outside but Hopper's dad wore a
purple singlet with a lot of red and grey curls
poking through the holes and among it all hung a
gynormous medallion. He was bald on top with
long ginger curls hanging down his back. Hopper
pushed the trolley full of beer bottles and bread.
Hopper's dad was ten foot high and fat with it.

'Dad, Dad, come here,' shouted Hopper,
pushing the trolley towards Lucy like a moth
after a turned-on light bulb.

89

We tried to run but got trapped by a mum trying to stop her three kids grabbing sweets at a separate check-out. She managed to stop two but a dirty little one with gold curls all over her head stuffed three Mars bars and a lollipop up her sweater. No one saw except me and she winked one big brown eye at me so I didn't see either. Besides, I'd got enough grief looking after Lucy and her sorrows.

Which were about to take a turn for the worse.

'I can't take much more,' she muttered to me. But she could. Hopper caught up with us.

'Dad, Dad, Dad. THIS is LUCY.'

Hopper made it sound as if Lucy was the Queen Mother, Marilyn Monroe, the Mona Lisa and Mary, the Queen of Heaven, all rolled into one.

We couldn't get away. His dad towered over us on his bow legs between us and the door.

'Look, look, Dad. She's wearing MY brooch!'

He wasn't gobbling. He was speaking so clearly you could hear it all over the super-market. Everyone seemed to be looking at us.

'Aarrh,' belched Hopper's dad. 'So you're little Lucy. You're Georgie's girl, then.'

On his face was what looked like a smile. Horrible it was. Knowing what Gowie had told me about him, I was not happy – in fact, I was getting less happy all the time. I've never liked supermarkets and this one was yuck. Lucy's gran was staring at us as if she couldn't believe it.

'George's girl,' repeated Hopper's dad. He stuck out his hand.

My gran shouted loudly and clearly, 'Marilyn – I can't wait all day! Gowie will be wanting his EVENING MEAL!'

'We can't keep Gowie waiting, can we?' beamed Marilyn, ringing everything in sight and waving like a castaway on a desert island spotting a ship.

It worked. A man trotted up to the cash till, looking important.

And I woke up.

I seized Hopper's dad's hand and shook it up and down.

'Lovely to meet you, Mr Hopper! Got to go. Sorry. See you tomorrow, George. Byeeeee!'

I dropped Hopper's dad's hand and grabbed Lucy's as I had once before.

'Run,' I hissed. And we ran out of the supermarket like rockets heading for the big black space of the car-park.

Later we sat drinking tea at the kitchen table at the Leadley-Browns'.

'Wish I could make it just Brown,' I muttered.

Gran kicked me under the table. 'Not yet,' she muttered back. Lost in their misery they didn't notice.

I'm so ashamed,' said Lucy's gran.

'Oh, don't be. It's such a waste of time. Besides, you came to our rescue the other night. Think of something nice, something important. Like what will you grow in the garden?'

'I'll tell you one thing,' I said.

'What's that?'

'Even if Hopper's awful, he's got good taste.'

'How's that?'

'He fancies Lucy. So he must have.'

She started to smile and then to giggle.

'I never thought that my first boyfriend would be somebody like Hopper.'

And then she put down her head and cried.

'Let her be,' said my gran. 'It'll do her good, poor lamb.'

Chapter Twelve

'Why did the one-armed man cross the road?'
'To get to the second-hand shop.'

Saturday market, late afternoon, the sky flaming red and orange, the church tower and the town roofs black against the blaze, a buzz in the air that grew colder every minute. There might be a frost, winter was on its way.

I was so alive I tingled: my toes tingled, my fingers tingled, sending out sparks, you could hear me crackle, wired up to I didn't know what. I wanted to jump, dance, fly, sing. I was wild as we wandered round the crowded jazzy stalls with their rainbow awnings, Daniella, Hannah, Natasha, Sue and me   WOW. Lights switched on, music played, my feet zipped, go, go, go, girl, dance, dance as we weaved through the crowds, looking, searching, everybody's looking for something, dreams, adventure, danger, here be dragons, here be wonders, and I was looking for a present for Gran, who'd got a birthday soon. I wanted something different, something SPECTACULAR. Surely I'd find it in these stalls crammed with goodies – jewellery, books, records, dresses, jeans, trainers, flowers, plants, antiques.

We'd been to a rehearsal, after which we had to go home, and we *were* going home, but taking the long way, through the market spilling over the pavements and into the graveyard of the old church, where they'd taken up the gravestones and stood them against the walls and put down seats for the wrinklies to sit on, with the stalls sprawling over the graveyard. At first they'd tried to stop people coming, but it was like trying to stop the tide, Gran said. So that now on this flaming late afternoon people were milling everywhere, people from miles around.

'All junk,' said Daniella, picking up butterfly earrings and dropping them down.

'Lovely junk!' I cried. 'I love it!'

'That's your gypsy great-grandmother. Loving all that tat!' She laughed.

'Yeah, that's it. I'll make wooden clothes-pegs and silk flowers, tie a scarf round my head and wear gold earrings, as big as . . .'

I drew a circle in the air and hit a woman pushing a couple of kids in a buggy.

'Watch it,' she shrieked. 'Hooligan!'

'Sorry, sorry,' I shouted, then we all fell about laughing.

'If you're a gypsy girl, tell my fortune,' shouted Natasha.

I seized her hand and pushed my face into it and chanted in a mysterious voice, 'You'll have a fantastic life. You'll marry a rich, handsome millionaire from Australia and have five children and twenty grandchildren!'

'Oh, no.' Giggle, giggle.

'Oh, yes. It's all there in the palm of your mitt, tra-la-la.'

'Go on. More!'

'Then your nose will drop off!'

'Oh, you. I'll get you.'

'Tell mine,' cried Daniella.

'No, no more . . .'

'Can you *really* tell fortunes?'

'Course not. It's only pretend.'

'Our fortunes are subject to the random chance of a chaotic universe . . .' announced Hannah.

'Oh, shut up,' we shouted. 'We're out of school.'

'You've got to tell mine,' cried Bossy Boots (Rich Boots) Daniella.

'OK, OK, but I've *got* to get Gran's present first. I want a funny one as well as a serious!'

So on we wandered round the stalls.

'Try this,' cried Natasha, holding up a Devil mask.

'No, no, no. It's horrible.'

95

'Or this,' said one of us and a tiger mask looked at us.

'No,' I screamed. 'Not that. Take it off!'

For a minute I didn't know which Cat it was. But it had to be Sue.

'Are you buying or what?' the stall-owner shouted.

'No,' we cried, threw the masks down and ran on.

'Kids,' he shouted after us.

Then I saw the umbrella stall.

'Stop. Let me look. She loses brollies all the time.'

We looked at every one of them. At last I bought a red one with black cats all over it, running, jumping, stretching, leaping.

'That's definitely the one,' Hannah said, so I knew it was.

I felt so extraordinary that afternoon. I didn't know whether to laugh or cry or fly to the moon. All of them probably. A whole wonderful world was all about us. Magic! Anything could happen and probably would.

A group of boys was following us now, watching, whispering, whistling, eyeing us up, especially Daniella, with her big blue eyes, her pink cheeks and her golden-fleece hair. We giggled and ran on, but she kept looking back at them.

'We're the Cricklepit Cats,' I called after them.

'Don't be so AWFUL,' giggled Natasha.

'We ought to be getting home. It's late,' Hannah said.

'I don't want to leave. Ever,' I cried.

'Zowey, you're wicked today. Just think of Mrs Leadley-Brown and control yourself.'

'I can't imagine her here.'

'She'd say how common it was. Markets, ugh!'

'Common as muck.'

'Unless it was in France. Then it would be so-oo WONDERFUL!'

'I can't imagine Lucy here either. She's so . . . so . . .'

'She's very nice,' said Hannah. 'I like her.'

'Stuck-up git,' said Natasha.

'Not really. It's just her way.'

We bought tapes, scrunchies, lipsticks, spending our money like crazy. I found a pair of huge earrings for Gran. They'd make her laugh. And a second-hand book of poems, red leather and gold, beautiful, real poems like she used to have to learn at school. I opened it.

> A bow-shot from her bower-eaves.
> He rode between the barley-sheaves
> The sun came dazzling thro' the leaves,
> And flamed upon the brazen greaves (the what?)
>> Of bold Sir Lancelot.

A red-cross knight for ever kneel'd
To a lady in his shield . . .

'Oh, come on, Zowey . . .'
'I'm coming. Wait for me . . .'
I opened another page.

Tiger, tiger burning bright
In the forests of the night . . .

No, no, not that. I didn't want Tigers or Tiro.
I ran on after the girls, as a cold wind stirred
suddenly, whipping round my feet.

But the sunset was mad, wild now, everything on fire. Dance, dance. I had to dance. I
must dance. There was a space. I dropped my
bag, lifted my arms above my head, clapped my
hands and danced. Somebody started to clap in
rhythm. The Cats ran towards me and joined
in, feet tapping, hands clapping, turning, turning, music playing. There was nothing in the
whole world but dancing. Then suddenly there
came another girl, her hands clapping, long
brown hair streaming and swirling round her
head. Lucy, it was Lucy. And we smiled and
danced on and on, hands, feet, hair turning
and moving to the beat – clap-clap-clap-clap.

'I'm the dancing queen,' I sang.

'We're the dancing queens,' we all sang,
holding hands, dancing for ever.

*

'Come on, come on. Break it up now, girls.'

Sergeant Price had arrived, no dancing queen, not him.

'Come on, now. Come on, Zowey Corby, stop showing off. Gowie's round here some-where, so stop making a spectacle of yourself. Come on, girls. Go home. It's getting late.'

We stopped dancing. The boys moved away. The watchers scattered slowly. I wanted to weep.

'Oh, yes, he was allowed to be bad. But I'm not, it's not fair!' I cried. But we turned for home all the same.

'Just let's have a Coke by the stall over there. Please. Before it all ends.' This was *actually* Lucy speaking. So we said OK and we were standing there drinking, when who should pop up out of the blue but Hopper with a huge red-silk flower for Lucy.

'Did you buy it?' she asked.

He shook his shaggy head.

'Then we'll put it back, shall we?'

She spoke very kindly and he nodded.

'Oh, Hopper,' said Natasha, but we went together and hid him as he put it back. And stayed with us. Naturally. All you've ever wanted, Hopper trailing along, but no one sent him away.

'Now,' said Daniella, Bossy Boots Daniella,

Rich Boots Daniella. 'Now you've got to tell MY fortune.'

'Oh, no, we're going home now.'

'Please, please, Zowey. Don't be a MEAN PIG! Tell my fortune!'

I took her hand.

'You'll be a pop star,' I began, and then I stopped, for the music crescendoed loud in my head and her hand shimmered and moved in mine and the lines in her hand interwove and spoke as clearly as clear to me:

'DANGER. DANGER.'

And I only like my danger in books and films. For you see – you see, though I can't tell fortunes to save my life, I do know a bit about it from Gran, who always says things like,

> 'Don't meddle,
> Don't dabble,
> Just leave it alone . . .'

And I can recognize the life line, which goes round the thumb and tells you (though I don't believe it) how long you'll live and when you'll be ill and when you'll die.

For as the lines settled, I could see Daniella's life line, and it broke in two just about NOW . . .

'Go on,' she shrieked. The music was playing very loudly now and I didn't like it any more. 'What's the matter?'

'Oh, nothing. You'll be beautiful and rich . . .' I managed.

'I'm that now!' Modest Daniella!

I felt terrible. What could I say?

'You'll – you'll have a Number One in the charts!'

'I'd rather find a cure for cancer,' put in Hannah.

'Or save the Third World,' from Sue.

'Oh, this is boring. Come on, let's go,' I cried.

'Zowey. ZOWEY. Tell me. About boys? MEN?' Daniella shrieked.

'What about them? There'll be hundreds.'

I ran on ahead.

For she wouldn't. She wouldn't have boys or men or anything else. Zilch. It all ended here. There'd be zilch for Daniella. And I was scared. I wanted Gran and Black Cat Cottage. I wished I'd never pretended to tell fortunes. I wished I'd never ever in a million years looked at Daniella's hand. The girls, Lucy as well, ran on and caught me up, the faithful Hopper lumbering behind. We hurried out of the market into the quieter streets, all of us silent now, all that fizz evaporated.

'Where's Daniella?' asked Hannah, stopping suddenly as she hurried beside me.

'With Sue. Just behind.'

'Oh, no, she's not.'

We gathered in a bunch. But not Daniella.

'She's still at one of the stalls.'

'Perhaps she's caught a bus. She's got further to go than the rest of us.'

'Or rang for someone to fetch her. You know what she's like.'

'She wouldn't not tell us, would she?'

PANIC.

'Zowey, what do you think?'

But Zowey wasn't thinking. This Zowey was screaming inside. She's dead. DEAD. Something's happened to her. She's been kidnapped. She's somewhere lying hurt. This is what I saw in her hand. This is it. Please God, help her, help us, please don't let her be dead, please keep her safe, keep her safe, keep her safe . . . PLEASE!

But I couldn't SAY a word.

We turned, ran back. Up and down, round and back, the others calling, 'Daniella, Daniella, Daniella.'

No answer. No one.

'She's lost,' whispered Natasha, face apple-green white. 'Someone's got her. You know what it's like. It's dangerous to be out. We should've gone home. My mother will kill me.'

'Seems you lose either way, Natasha,' murmured Sue.

'We'll find Sergeant Price,' Hannah said. 'He'll find her. She's probably quite safe.'

We ran this way and that way, searching. I could see her hand – that awful life line that broke – oh, why had I danced and been so happy? I should have known. But I didn't want to know. How could I know? Please God, I prayed, please Jesus, keep her safe, please Mary, take care of her. And I'll never, never pretend to tell fortunes again.

'Don't any of the rest of us get lost,' cried Hannah. 'Keep together.'

'It's really dark now.'

'And cold.'

> 'We're the Cricklepit Cats.
> And we don't care.
> And we're not afraid,' sang Hannah
> quaveringly.

'Yes, we are. Scared stiff,' squeaked Natasha.

We'd drawn together in a bunch, afraid to be alone, calling, 'Daniella! Daniella!'

It wasn't Daniella who shot up in front of us but Gowie, frowning, brown eyes black and red when he's angry.

'What are you lot doing here? Get home. It's late. What's the matter? What are you crying for, Natasha? No, not all of you at once.'

Natasha poured words out . . .

'I can't follow that. Zowey. Hannah. Tell me.'

We told him.

'You crazy gits. If you must go round a market at this time of night, just stay together.'

He stuck two fingers in his mouth and whistled. They came from all over in minutes. At least ten of them. Gowie's mates. The Corby Gang. I knew them all. Some even Mrs L-Brown would approve of, but there were three or four Gran wouldn't let in through the door. Unless you nailed everything down, including the fireplace, she said.

What Gowie said at machine-gun speed sounded like a foreign language, and they shot off in different directions. He turned to us.

'Now, you. Home.'

I hate him when he comes over Bossy Male Pig, even though I was glad he was there.

'We can't go. Not yet.'

'Well, wait in this caff. And stay put together. Yeah. Please. I don't want to search for any more of you.'

The caff was scruffy. I'd not been there before. I flopped down, gone beyond. Hannah gathered in some money and she and Lucy ordered. Lucy ate a hot dog. Hopper ate two.

'How can you?' Natasha was still crying. 'When poor Daniella is lying dead . . .'

This was rather how I felt, only hearing Natasha say it made it less likely somehow. Daniella couldn't be dead, not all that bounce and show-off and tendril hair, could she? No.

'I think she's picked up one of those boys,' Hannah said.

'No–ooo,' gobbled Hopper, through tomato sauce all over his mouth and chin and dribbling on to his T-shirt. 'T-t-iro.'

'Tiro!' I shouted, coming to life. 'You saw her with Tiro!'

'Mmmmmmm,' he grunted, shoving his second hot dog in at one go.

'Hopper, why didn't you tell us?' asked Lucy.

'Nobody-mmm-grunt-grunt-asked me,' gobbled Hopper.

Two minutes later Gowie's gang arrived, Daniella and Tiro in the midst of it, Daniella tear-stained, not Rich Bossy-Boots any more, Tiro whistling.

'They were at the jewellery stall. It's a wonder we didn't have to get them out of the police station, 'cos we only just got to them before Sergeant Price, me old schoolmate. Now, Tiro, are you carrying any rings and things, any drugs, anything you shouldn't have?'

The gang closed in on Tiro as Daniella came over to finish the Coke I couldn't.

'I'm clean as a whistle. Pure as a new-born babe.' Tiro grinned, opening his hands to show they were empty.

'Daniella,' I said. 'Let me see *your* hand again. You see, I was worried about you.'

I looked at her palm. There wasn't really much of a break in the life line. But I said, 'Take care. It's funny here.'

'Oh. I expect that's last year. That car crash. Don't you remember? I was in hospital for a week . . . I'm all right, Zowey, *honest*. I'll have those hundred boyfriends yet.'

'Stay here,' yelled Gowie. 'I'll get the Jag and drive you all home in style.'

'It'll never make it,' shouted someone, but a cheer went up just the same.

Chapter Thirteen

'Take me up to the top of the city'
Kate Bush, 'Top of the City'

Rosie collected Lucy and me to help her deliver
leaflets – saving children and saving seals –
both at the same time. She always goes over the
top. We went down to the quay and along by
the river.

'I haven't been here much,' said Lucy. 'We
always went abroad in the holidays. Or I was at
school.'

'Poor you. I'll show you the city,' Rosie
grinned.

So we rode round on mini-buses looking at
ancient buildings and church spires and shops,
for the minis can go through the city centre. We
got out near the cathedral and walked round
the great building, looking at the tombs and
reading the monuments. I showed her my two
favourites, the skeleton tomb and chapel with
little owls carved all over it. She liked the owls.

At last we emerged.

'I need a coffee,' Rosie said first.

'Please may I see where Hopper lives. The "other" country. But I don't want him to see me. Can we do that?'

'You're crazy. But come on. Off to Hopper's Stately Home.'

We caught another mini to the estate where Hopper lives. It looked just the same as ever. Awful. But Lucy gazed at it as if it were New York or Mexico City – something strange and exotic. Boarded-up windows and graffiti were new to her, I supposed. She didn't speak, but then Lucy doesn't much. We got out just before Hopper's bit, Nightingale Road. Hopper lives at Number 13. Well, he would, wouldn't he?

We stared at the boarded-up windows and a front garden full of crates of empties and old black sacks the local cats had torn up at a midnight party.

'Oh,' she said. We walked on a bit, trying to keep out of sight. Then she stopped.

'Oh, dear,' she said, looking round.

I pulled at her. 'Hurry up! Look, there's a load of little kids trailing us. Let's go.'

'Yes, let's hurry up,' Rosie said, 'if you don't want to see Hopper.'

We walked faster. So did the kids, singing and kicking balls by this time.

'Just round the corner. I'll catch you up. I've got three more leaflets for this street.'

And at that moment, 'Lucy! Lucy! Lucy!' rang through the air.

It was Hopper. And about twenty little kids who all began to shout, 'Lucy! Lucy! Juicy Lucy! Lucy, Juicy Lucy!'

She flushed bright red. We ran. And ran and ran and ran. At last the noise faded, for Hopper's fat and the kids are little. We stood at a corner and waited for Rosie, who took ten minutes to find us as she'd taken another route. Naturally we found a caff and fell in, shattered.

After a bit we recovered, helped by dough-nuts and warm drinks. Lucy sat back firmly (looking like her grandma, as she does every now and then).

'*Now*. I want to see where Tiro lives.'

'Oh, no. It's miles out in the country. Some big old place, I think. No one's ever been out there. And he's got a computer he's mad about. He's brilliant on the computer, you must've noticed.'

We walked on further.

'He's not poor, then?' asked Lucy.

'No, not at all,' said Rosie. 'But they're mad. His father's very peculiar. No one goes there because he's got guns and things. He's a law unto himself. He's very harsh with Tiro, they say.'

'But why does Tiro hang round with Hopper in town? Why does he come to this school?'

'Don't ask me. Who knows why Tiro does anything? I think he was expelled from the one he was at that was nearer,' Rosie said.

'Oh, that was ages ago. He's been in our class for yonks, messing about,' I said, bored. 'Can we go now? I hope we don't have to go and look at Tiro's house, Lucy. We'd probably get shot. What do you want to know for, anyway?'

'Oh, I'm interested in finding out about you all.'

'Nosy Parker, heh?'

'Come on,' said Rosie. 'There's just a few more leaflets left. Can you keep going?'

'Oh, yes, I love it, ha, ha. But I'll stay with you, even if it kills me.'

We separated off to get rid of the leaflets faster. Left on my own, I popped two or three in doors and some behind hedges, because I've been doing this for years and years and I'm not noble like Rosie Lee. And as I walked on and up the hills and round and round the houses and streets, I kept singing an absolutely gross song that kept going round and round in my brain – you know how it is.

So to get rid of it I started going through the week at school. Lots of rehearsals for *The Jungle*

Book now. Karem, a boy from year five was Mowgli. Sue was Kaa, the rock python; Roland, King of the Monkeys. Sir chose Lucy for Bagheera – a big part (Juicy Lucy, said Tiro, just like the kids in Nightingale Road). And Hopper was Hathi, the King of the Elephants. Everyone thought Sir had gone bonkers.

'He may *look* the part. BUT . . .'

But Hopper loved it and was rehearsing every spare minute. He glowed, said Mrs Thomson.

'So do glow-worms,' muttered Tiro.

He was black, blacker than black – moody, eyes wild. I told Gran about it.

'It'll all end in tears, I expect,' she said. 'Not to worry, Zowey. Just keep on with the practising.'

For I had a flute solo in the play. It scared me but made me feel great as well. Natasha and Hannah were playing their clarinets. Daniella was Sir's personal assistant, designing costumes and scenery.

Matthew was Shere Khan. They did try Tiro, who looked perfect for the part – typecasting, said Mr Merchant – but now here's what rocked the school last week and thinking of it soon sent the silly song out of my brain.

Tiro mucked about at rehearsals – he always does – and kept winding up Hopper – sneering

and jeering at him as Hathi. Hopper, no longer
Tiro's slave, but really chuffed to be in the play
and acting with Lucy, managed to ignore him till
Tiro started to say some really vile things about
them both – too disgusting to repeat – and he
pushed Hopper who, caught off balance, fell
over on to Lucy – and Hopper, who's no light-
weight, bumped her arm in the scuffle. Percy
intervened and was attacked by Tiro, whose eyes
were completely wild now and features going
everywhere, sliding off his face.

'You can't touch me,' yelled Tiro. 'It's against
European law.'

Percy did touch him. He dragged him off to
the headteacher's room. Mrs Thomson then
took over, calmed us all down and gave Shere
Khan's part to Matthew.

Tiro was suspended for a week. The story of
Tiro is like a soap – what will happen next? But
then . . . so is school. The trouble with Tiro is
there's always the feeling it will, as Gran says,
all end in tears . . . or . . . even worse.

I was reaching the top of the hill now where the
streets of houses opened out to the big ones
with their long drives and surrounding trees.

Rosie and Lucy joined me.

'You worked hard, Zowey,' Rosie said.
'You've got rid of all yours.'

I didn't tell her why. I sometimes don't think I'm *naturally* good. But happy.

We carried on up the hill. I did some of Lucy's. We were a bit tired now. And cold.

'Gosh, it's steep,' I said.

'We've nearly finished. There's only a few left.' Rosie pushed me on up from behind.

'You and your leaflets. I've been delivering leaflets for you all my life.'

'Not for me. For anyone or anything that needs help. Remember.'

'Do they do any good, I wonder?'

'You must keep trying, Zowey.'

'Oh shut up, Rosie. No wonder Gowie gets fed up with you at times. You're too good to live. No, sorry, I don't mean that.'

'My gran wouldn't allow leaflets to be delivered. She had a notice on the gate saying, "No Hawkers, Circulars, Tradesmen". That's when she lived on her own. Now she's changed. She's into everything. She had me collecting for the Aged the other evening. It was dark and I was scared,' said Lucy.

'Do you think I'm too do-goody for Gowie?' asked Rosie suddenly, looking worried.

'No, I don't mean it,' I said quickly. 'He loves you, honest.'

'Oh, I don't know. I love him but he'll always go after other girls. And he doesn't believe in the things I believe in. Oh, Zowey!'

'Don't worry.' What else could I say? Besides,
I was puffed out. I wanted to go home as the
streets went on and on. We fell silent and I
noticed Lucy looking round her in a peculiar
way. Was something wrong? I turned to ask her
but I was too tired. And lost, but we were
nearly at the top now. We plodded on. The top
house? Very grand. A far cry and a long way
from Hopper's. No, there was yet another
behind it. The city lay far below us now as I
turned round to Lucy and saw the tears streaming down her face. I could just see another
house further on behind the trees and bushes,
beautiful even in winter. Lucy ran towards it.

'I didn't know we were coming here,' she
sobbed.

We ran after her. For there was the grey
stone house of Lucy's photograph. Her Tara.
Gone With the Wind. Dream country.

'Oh, Lucy. I'm so sorry. Oh, what an idiot I
am,' cried Rosie.

We stood huddled together under the trees,
for it was turning bitterly cold. Winter had
arrived, everywhere. And was settling in Lucy's
heart. We waited with her as she wept. And at
last took her back to Black Cat Lane and home.

Chapter Fourteen

'Here is a box, a musical box,
And inside it has a secret to tell,
But can you guess that secret?'

Lucy's room was beautiful now – white curtains
at the window, cream painted floor, books, a
patchwork quilt, a radio and tape-recorder, a
poster of James Dean and a painting of a road
going up a hill with a tree beside a hedge. It
made me want to cry, I didn't know why. It
also made me think I ought to clean up mine.
Perhaps Beatrix Potter, a torn poster of Meat-
Loaf and three pairs of old roller-skates had
passed their sell-by date.

We sat as we had before, like bookends in the
window-seat, now clean and painted white like
the room. And she sat, hair over her face, not
speaking once. And yet it wasn't the same as
before. She was my friend now and I was hers.

Downstairs Rosie was helping Mrs Leadley-
Brown paint the kitchen. She'd helped her a lot.
So had Gowie, believe it or not. Lucy ran, not

speaking, to her room at the top and I followed, not that I knew what I had to do or say but I knew I had to be there. For she was my friend now and I was hers.

She sat silent, being a girl who could say nothing for ages.

At last, 'Tell me if you want to,' I said. I didn't look at *her* but out over the view, the steep embankments, the Wild Patch with its branches, bare now and Black Cat tunnel.

'Black! Black!' she said. 'It was like that black tunnel. But you didn't have any choice. You'd got to go into it. One minute the sun shone and then you were in the blackness, just like that. You kept wanting to turn everything back to yesterday.'

I went cold inside. After a bit she went on.

'Everything turned upside-down. Twisted out of shape. What was good was bad and what you'd trusted and believed in was a lie. I'd gone into the dark.'

She held out her hands and looked at them, the fingers outstretched. She seemed to be recording them for ever as if she'd never seen them before and wondered how they came to be there.

'The people you loved didn't love you. Or not enough.'

'Oh, Lucy.'

'Don't cry, Zowey. It's bad enough me doing it all the time.

116

'They kept saying I was a good girl. What a good girl Lucy is, they said, over and over again. She's so sensible. All I wanted to do was scream, scream, scream, scream – No, no, I don't want this. I want the sun again, not the darkness. I'm not going to be sensible. I'm going to scream for ever.'

She continued, ' "Have you got a hankie?" the solicitor said, Daddy's friend. "OF COURSE I HAVEN'T GOT A HANKIE!" I yelled. "WHAT DO YOU THINK? MY DAD EMBEZZLED – THAT'S THE FANCY WORD FOR STOLEN – LOTS OF OTHER PEOPLE'S MONEY AND WHEN HE WAS FOUND OUT HE SHOT HIMSELF . . .'

'Oh, no, Lucy.'

'Oh, yes, Zowey. "AND MY MOTHER COULDN'T STAND THE DISGRACE OR WANT TO STAY WITH ME SO SHE'S RUN OFF WITH DADDY'S BEST FRIEND. I'VE NO FATHER, NO MOTHER, NO HOME, NO DOG, NO PONY – NOT ANY MORE. EVERYTHING I HAD'S BEEN TAKEN OFF ME. WHAT MAKES YOU THINK THEY'VE LEFT ME A HANKIE?" He didn't know what to say, the solicitor, Daddy's friend.'

'Your gran?' I sobbed. 'Where does she come in?'

'Oh, she came in like the US cavalry in a cowboy film. Told me to quit carrying on and crying and get on with it. Daddy had taken her money too. "We're starting off together and we'll make a go of it," she said. But I didn't want to make a go of it. I just wanted to die.'

'Yes.'

'She did everything, my gran. Sorted it all out. While I walked in the dark.'

'What about your friends?'

'Mum and Dad's friends either vanished or didn't speak or sued us. My friend Candia . . .'

'Oh, the toothpaste girl!'

'Yeah, that's right. She and Sally came. They wanted to know if it was all true. They wanted to hear all the details. They – they seemed to like it. They did keep coming to see me for a bit, then I think their mothers stopped them. Sally had the pony. I didn't like that because she's not very nice with animals, but it did mean I could see him. But then that stopped as well. In what they call the summer holiday, everything stopped . . .'

'Surely you could've kept the dog!'

'He was old and everyone said he'd miss the big garden. So he was put down. My gran tried to stop them but they took him when she was out. Said it was best for him and me. No reminders were best, they said.'

Fury stood me up on the window-seat.

'Who are these "they" people? These beasts – these creatures – who are they?'

'Oh, people. They come, you know. The solicitors, the receivers, the doctor, oh, people all helping me, they said. They found the house for us and the school. They kept saying how much they wanted to help me and Grandma. Then they went away. I think we . . . embarrassed them. My father had done wrong things, you see. So we must be wrong too.'

'No – no, you aren't,' I shouted. 'You're straight and true and brave. Much better and braver than me. But if they come here I shall kill those people! I shall slaughter them and chop them into bits!'

I stamped with rage.

'Oh, horrible old world that has such people in it,' I cried to the view outside, to the birds in the air and the clouds in the sky. My eyes hurt with all the tears. And it was Lucy calming me down, saying don't mind, it's all right, they didn't mean it, they thought they were helping. I shook with tears – happy girl, Zowey – the tears that would never really go away. But why, why was I crying so, feeling such pain? This had happened to Lucy, not me. But it was all our pain. Mrs Thomson had read us something about no one being an island and everyone's grief affecting all of us. Yes, but there was something further inside me still. And thinking of Mrs Thomson reminded me of her saying that it was fine to draw the curtains on your mind as long as what was hidden didn't catch up with you one day. Had it caught up with me now?

Lucy reached for my hand and pulled me down on to the seat.

'We're the same really. It must have happened to you. Once you had a mother and father who went away. And you have a grandma too – like me.'

'But you're grand and I'm just a gypsy girl, really!'

'That's stupid and you know it, Zowey. Besides, who you are doesn't make any difference to how you feel! But at least you have Gowie!'

I'd stopped crying. I could manage a joke, just a little one – not very good.

'Well, you've got Hopper. You weren't to know Handsome Prince Hopper was waiting for you!'

'No, I didn't guess it could be that bad!'

I borrowed the famous hankie and dried my eyes. Better now.

'What did that Candia Toothpaste say about our school?'

'Oh, awful things, like I told you. And I

believed her. That's why I was in such a state when I came. I'm sorry. I didn't know how nice you all were.'

'Even Tiro and Hopper?'

'Knowing them has helped me somehow. You know, not long ago I saw them . . .'

'Those, those girls? Candia and Thing?'

'Yes. They were walking along with two of the teachers, Boo and Banksie we called them. Everyone had crushes on them 'cos they weren't as dreary as the others.'

'Boo and Banksie! What stupid names! What did they say to you?'

'They sort of nodded, then rushed on as if they were late for a train or something. They looked SILLY. And I wondered how I'd ever cared about anything they said.'

'Hooray. Are you OK, Lucy?'

'Yeah.' She rubbed the window. 'Let's go downstairs and get some grub.'

She rubbed the window harder.

'Zowey, Zowey. Look. There's a train going through. Slowly. On the other track, away from the station. Can you see it?'

'Yes.'

'Well, there's somebody on the roof. Is it – is it – Tiro?'

'Yes, oh, Lord, yes, he's riding the train. And Hopper's down there watching him!'

Chapter Fifteen

'The tigers of wrath are wiser than the horses of
  destruction'

William Blake

Under the laurel bush, over the fence, over the
barbed wire, sliding, bumping, half falling,
panting, shrieking, we arrived there, splat,
down at the bottom of the Wild Patch cliff.

We'd been there before. Then it was leafy
autumn. Now it was December.

'But what are we going to do?' gasped Lucy.

'I dunno. But I do know we've gotta stop Tiro
before he gets himself killed.'

When we got down beside the rail track there
was no sign of Tiro or Hopper. We ran up and
down beside the gritted track calling them, till
Lucy said, 'Somebody might spot *us* and report
us for trespassing!'

'That'd be a laugh!'

'I wish Gowie would come this time. He'd
know what to do.'

She ran one way, I ran the other, still calling.

Where had Hopper gone? And Tiro? The little train Tiro was riding had come from the main station towards the Halt, where people got off for the City football ground and shops at the top of the steep embankments. This little train stopped at several small stations till it linked up with the main line at a junction further on.

We slowed down and joined up again.

'This is useless.'

'What are we doing here?'

'If Tiro wants to get himself killed it's his worry!'

'Don't be horrible, Zowey. You know you don't mean it.'

'Don't I? He's always causing trouble. Now we've got to climb up that terrible bank again.'

'Let's have one more look, then go.'

'Tiro must've jumped down before he reached the Halt or he'd be spotted . . .'

'Not if he lay absolutely flat.'

'But you can't miss Hopper. He sticks out a mile.'

'That's his stomach.'

We giggled and cheered up. After all, I thought, here we are. Danger, danger. The banks swooped down, winter grey sky above. It was all very spectacular.

'We could be in a film.'

More confident now, we ran into the tunnel,

keeping well to the side. It was light at first, then grew darker and we slowed down. It smelt sooty, strange. And grew darker still. A finger of fear poked at me and all the hairs down my back stood up under my clothes and I shivered.

'It's cold. Let's go back,' whispered Lucy.

'Yeah. I'm tired. And cold.'

I was. What a day! All that leaflet-delivering, seeing the city, Hopper's house, seeing Lucy's Tara and hearing her sad story. Now this. The day had lasted for ever. I was cold, hungry and tired. And also scared. Fear came again, trotting beside us in the tunnel along with the dark.

'Lucy. Let's turn round and go back now.'

'Yes. We're being silly. Right. Now one more time. Hopper! Hopper! Hopper! Tiro!'

A voice from the blackness whispered, 'They aren't here. But we are!' and we were grabbed. Bodies were all around us in the dark, our arms were seized – pushing, banging.

I was hauled off my feet but, before a hand came over my mouth I managed to shriek, 'No, no, help!'

They dragged us, kicking and struggling uselessly, to where it was lighter, not out of the tunnel, but nearer the edge. Right at the back of my head a voice that was like Gowie's was saying, 'What are all these crazy gits doing wandering round in a railway tunnel?' But then

I smelt whoever was holding me and terror took over, panic waves, sweat, trembling, a roaring in my ears almost louder than what they were saying.

'It's Corby's kid. Well, well. He owes me, stuck-up bastard!'

'And the Posh Git.'

'Corby's sister and friends of the Black Cow.'

'Lucky find. Treasure.'

'And alone. Great.'

'What are you two doing down here? Looking for . . .'

What he said was so vile I didn't think Lucy would understand, but the waves of terror were blanking out my brain. I tried to remember what Gowie had taught me and I kicked backwards sharply and bit the hand that held my mouth, scratched and clawed.

'Gowie,' I managed to scream, and was slapped back and forwards across my face.

'Pity Black Cow isn't here too.'

'We can have enough fun with these two. Long hair. See!'

Please save us. Please send Gowie, I prayed. He didn't come.

They were tearing my sweater. I heard a muffled groan from Lucy. We were lost, done for. What a thing to happen. Just how stupid could you get. What were you doing down there?

they'd say. If we ever got out of here.

I ached. I was bruised. I couldn't fight much more. Lucy had sunk down on the track. Then I was down on the track too. Suppose a train came. But I wished a train would come – we'd be killed – but I thought they'd kill us anyway – people are killed and they don't think it will be them – I didn't think anything really would happen to Lucy – and – me – oh, Gran!

'Help!' I heard Lucy yell.

And from the dark of the tunnel behind us now sounded lumbering footsteps – bump, bump, bump – echoing and re-echoing.

'Lucy, Lucy. I'm coming!'

Hopper wasn't gobbling. Hopper was yelling clearly as he ran towards us.

And I could remember Gowie saying, 'Don't cross Hopper's dad. Ever. Wrestling champion in his heyday. Before the beer got him.'

Funny thing to remember. Hopper would be useless against this lot. But a bit of strength returned and I fought back again as Hopper, grunting like a wild pig, charged into the midst of the gang, fists and feet flying with a power no one could've guessed at.

They were too much for us. I hurt – oh, I hurt. What would they do to us? But I knew what they would do to us. And I was afraid. The dark tunnel had turned into hell. This was like some awful horror film and I didn't want to be in it.

And there sounded the roar of a train approaching . . .

'Back, back, against the walls!'

I bit, then screamed and screamed.

Chaos. The train came nearer, huge for a little train. We were all going to be killed!

'Shove 'em under the train,' shouted one of them. But we were crushed back against the wall as someone dropped silently from the train roof, a phantom almost in the gloom, straight on to the one holding me. Then I lay back, eyes shut, as the train rumbled through drowning shouts and screams.

My captor had dropped me and was fighting Tiro.

'Run,' he yelled as pandemonium broke loose – muddle, confusion.

Suddenly, as quickly as they'd appeared, the gang vanished, leaving Lucy, Hopper and me, with Tiro lying on the track, his head covered in blood.

Chapter Sixteen

'What of the hunting, hunter bold?'
    'Brother, the watch was long and cold.'
'What of the quarry ye went to kill?'
    'Brother, he crops in the jungle still.'
'What of the strength that was your pride?'
    'Brother, it ebbs from my flank and side.'
'Where is the haste that ye hurry by?'
    'Brother, I go to my lair – to die.'
        Rudyard Kipling *The Jungle Book*

We thought Tiro would die. He lay on the track
and there was a lot of blood. I know from first
aid you're not supposed to move people, but
we couldn't leave him there so we got him to
the side of the railway lines – at least Hopper
did – and then he went up that awful bank and
fetched help, while I sat with Tiro's head on my
lap and he bled and we covered him with our
clothes and Hopper had left his anorak – it was
old and smelt of sweat and fish and chips and it
was comforting – and Lucy and me, we put our
arms round each other and Tiro, and wrapped

the anorak round us, for it was cold and we couldn't stop trembling. And waited till Hopper came with everybody.

I still tremble and I still live the tunnel over and over again. And so does Lucy. It will be better later on, Gran says. Give it time. Lucy is braver about it than me. But then she is. Braver, I mean.

Blanket is there when I have nightmares. Black cat Blanket, fat, warm, sleepy, my comforter. We're getting Lucy a kitten so she can have it on her bed in the night – if Grandma Leadley-Brown agrees, and I think she will.

We had some days off school, missing the parties – sad – and the opting-in-out-meeting. It was a very wild and noisy meeting apparently. Gran and Rosie told me all about it and the vote went *against* opting out. Gran and Rosie were delighted, drinking a bottle of wine together with GL-B.* She'd voted the other way but sank a bottle with them all the same. She's going to be a school governor. Gowie was busy somewhere else – and I knew where and who he was with, but I'm not telling Rosie. If he wasn't Gowie, I'd – I'd splatter him.

I got all these cards. They're all round my bed, together with all the flowers and chocs and

*Grandma Leadley-Brown.

paperbacks Gowie brought in. Gran said he was off his rocker. But none of the cards was as HUGE as Lucy's. It was about the size of a door – from Hopper, of course.

'Glory alleluia, how VULGAR,' shrieked GL-B when it came, Lucy told me. And then, 'But how sweet.' Hopper was invited to tea. I wish I'd been there. Lucy just stuck her nose in the air and wouldn't tell me about it when I asked – mean thing. 'Next time, you've *got* to invite me,' I said, 'and then I can watch.'

'No way. There won't be a NEXT time, anyway.'

So I mimicked her posh voice and she got mad.

Rosie came.

'Gowie's out,' I said.

'I've come to see you and Lilian.'

And she told us she'd volunteered to go to Africa to help with refugee work.

'That's not because of Gowie, is it?' asked Gran sharply. 'Because if it is, it won't work out for you.'

'No, you know I want to go. I can't stay and do nothing while children suffer. You know that. And I'm eighteen now, so it's time. I have to go.'

I cried a bit and Gran kissed her.

What she and Gowie said I don't know. I wasn't there. I wasn't caring much about *him* – I didn't want Rosie to go and he was the only one who could stop her. But he wouldn't, would he?

We went back to school for the dress rehearsals.

In the afternoon Mrs Thomson gave out our reports and read out bits from the stories we'd written.

Hannah had written about the Middle Ages, Matthew about football, Daniella about Disneyland, Hopper had made up a poem for Lucy – mainly, I love Lucy – and Sue's was the best, I thought. She'd written down all the funny bits and pieces and things that the customers said in her dad's shop and called it 'Flied Lice'.

But Lucy won. She'd written about 'A New Life in a New School', and it was wonderful and clever and a shock, because we hadn't realized that while we were registering *her*, she'd been registering us.

'I thought your account excellent,' Mrs Thomson said to Lucy. 'Have you got any future plans?'

I think she meant, 'Are you going to stay here?'

'When I grow up I'll have my own school and I won't have any trouble in it and all my children will be happy,' she said.

131

'You mean like your old school?' Hannah said.

'Oh, no. Not wet and boring like that. But sort of tough and orderly.'

It was the first time we'd heard her criticize her old school. Sue was winking and grinning.

'You've written about our school. But what do you really like best?' Mrs Thomson asked.

'Oh, the music. Learning to play the clarinet. And *The Jungle Book*. I feel wonderful when it all gets going. And I love my part.'

'But what about the boys?' asked Matthew. 'You didn't mention them in your story.'

'What about the boys?' She grinned. 'Well, I like you all *really*.'

So we laughed.

'Very good, Lucy,' Mrs Thomson said. 'You've settled well.'

I sat waiting.

'Where did yours get to, Zowey?'

I didn't answer.

'What's the matter? You didn't have to do it. But you seemed so keen. Come on, Zowey. What went wrong? You can tell us.'

'I don't want to finish it. I don't like it any more. I read Lucy's when she didn't know and it was better than mine. I wanted my story to be about danger and romance, which I've always wanted stories to be about. But now I know I'm scared of danger, and romance is horrible boys in tunnels and sitting frozen while Tiro is dying. I'd rather play my flute. So there!'

And I got up and ran out of school.

'She isn't better yet,' they all said and were so *nice* to me that it made me sick. For it wasn't that. But I didn't know what it was.

'I think you drew those curtains in your mind back a bit,' said Mrs Thomson when I went back next day and said sorry.

'I will finish it. Now it's not in a competition. I don't like competitions, you see.'

'Yes, I do see.'

'I want to see Tiro,' I said.

'I'll take you,' said Gowie.

They said Tiro was in intensive care and we'd heard awful things – he was brain-damaged, he would be a vegetable, he would have to go to prison, no one could visit him.

I walked in behind Gowie – terrified. But then Tiro had always frightened me. He'd saved me, but if he hadn't been train-riding I wouldn't have been down there having to be saved anyway! I wanted to run. But I had to come. If I saw him, the nightmares and trembles might go away. I clutched a huge bunch of grapes and chocolates. I hope he likes grapes, I thought. He was in a ward on his own. And he was asleep.

I was so glad. His mad, sad blue eyes with eyelashes like car-washers always scared me.

'Hi,' Gowie said.

He opened his eyes and saw me. I held out my gifts and waited.

'Hi, Zowey, Florence Nightingale,' he said in an ordinary sort of voice.

Relief swept over me in great waves. I had to sit down. It was all so *ordinary*. His eyes were clear, steady. I smiled into them. They weren't mad.

'Hi, Tiro.'

'Hey, Gowie. D'you think you could rustle up a computer for me?'

'I'll see what I can do,' promised Gowie.

Chapter Seventeen

'Bear necessities! That's all we need, Zowie!'
Lucy Leadley-Brown

Outside the wind moaned and howled like
someone being tortured, as it lifted dustbins
over walls, snatched tiles off roofs and snapped
branches off trees. This wind had blown all
day. But inside our new school theatre the
lights were bright and people came despite the
weather. WE/US the orchestra were tuning up.
I was a panther in black sweater and leggings, a
black tail, black velvet ears on a hair band. For
all the musicians were jungle animals seated
among palm trees. The costumes were brill,
fabulous, fantastic. Kaa wore a sea-green shim-
mering leotard, a snake's head and mask and a
metres-long chiffon tail which she swirled to
perfection. I can't say which was the most
wonderful – Karem as Mowgli, Shere Khan's
facepaint, Bagheera in black velvet! Maybe –
just maybe – Elephant Hathi (Hopper) topped
the lot. For end-of-term school plays are magic.

All the rehearsal cock-ups faded away and brilliance shone instead, with the acting and the dancing and the singing and the music.

The wind outside seemed miles away. Gran sat by Lucy's grandma and Rosie with Gowie. All week they had been talking, arguing and not happy, but now they smiled and waved at me.

'Funny to do *The Jungle Book* at Christmas!' I heard someone say to Mr Merchant as we settled in our places.

'Makes a change from old Scrooge, and Ye Olde Victorian Times,' he chortled. 'Wider horizons, y'know.'

After that everything faded and there was nothing in the whole world but the lights, the play, the music, the dancing, the colours, the glory, the glamour. If I'd had wings I'd have flown all round the little theatre. As it was, I played my flute as if I could never stop.

'You were great,' Sir said to Lucy and me in the interval, 'especially after a tough time. Supertroupers!'

'Heroines. We're heroines, Sir,' I said with a straight face.

'Oh, yes, you always wanted to be a heroine, Zowey! Hopper's a heroine, too. Very pretty heroine, George.'

'Do you always joke, Sir?' asked Lucy. She's got used to men teachers now, she'd told me in one of our long chats.

'Yes.' He grinned.

'Even if you were being tortured. Or dying?'

'In those extreme circumstances both the jokes and I would be a bit weak, I expect, Lucy, but we'd do our best.'

Then we were back with the music, the lights, the colour, the dazzle.

At last, after the applause and the cheering, the bowing and the bouquets, the audience rose to go, still humming and smiling, and made their way to the doors.

And suddenly the wind that had gusted all evening seemed to blow right in with us, around us and above us. It was so loud we clapped our fingers to our ears. Terrifying.

'Look out!' shouted a voice. 'The windows are shattering!' Someone else screamed.

Head Fred, Mrs Thomson and Sir were suddenly there, ushering people slowly outside . . .

But it wasn't the windows.

In the light thrown by the school and the streetlamps we could see leaves and branches everywhere. The wind dropped suddenly.

'The old tree's down,' cried a voice. 'Take care.'

'Just one of the branches,' shouted Head Fred.

'It's on someone's car.'

People struggled and milled round. We'd all streamed outside in our costumes to see everything, for it was fairly calm now, a lull in the storm.

People began to haul debris away to see what damage had been done.

'It's just one big branch blown off.'

'On somebody's car.'

'A red Jag by what you can see of it.'

'It's pretty smashed.'

Gowie pushed forward. 'A red Jag, you say?'

'As far as I can tell.'

'It's mine,' groaned Gowie. He went up to it, pushing all the little leaves and branches aside. 'Yes, it's mine all right. Squashed like a concertina.'

'Keep still, everyone,' said Sergeant Price. 'Then we can organize things so you can all drive away. The rest are all right, I think. We'll ring the breakdown services for you, Gowie.'

'Gowie,' Gran whispered in all the din, but I could hear. 'Was it insured?'

'Course it wasn't,' he replied. 'You know me.'

'Yes, I do. Why did you bring it?'

'Because it was windy, of course. Oh, shut up, I'll have to get going.'

Back at home later, Gran sat in the kitchen. She looked very sad.

'Are you worrying about him?'

'No,' she said. 'No, it's the tree. It'll have to come down now.'

'Well, it's just a tree coming down.'

She smiled at me and poured herself a glass of something to join the tea.

'No. You won't understand, Zowey, but it's the end of an era. My youth gone.' She almost looked as if she were going to cry, but she didn't. Gran hardly ever cries.

This was a bit much for me so I went up to bed to find Blanket, and to finish the story.

THE END

The Turbulent Term of Tyke Tiler

by Gene Kemp

Tyke Tiler is very fond of jokes – that's why there are so many in this story. And Tyke is also fond of Danny Price, who is not too bright and depends a lot on his friend. In fact, medium bright Tyke and medium dim Danny add up to double trouble, especially during their last term at Cricklepit Combined School.

Gowie Corby Plays Chicken

by Gene Kemp

Gowie Corby is the terror of Cricklepit Combined School. He's mean, and he wants no help and no friends – apart from Boris Karloff, his pet rat. So when an ancient cellar is uncovered at the school, with ghosts and all, nothing is surely going to prevent him from spending a night there. Especially when he'll be called chicken if he doesn't.

Charlie Lewis Plays for Time

by Gene Kemp

For Charlie Lewis and his friends in class 4M, the last term of Cricklepit Combined School *could* have been fun. That is, if the beloved Mr Merchant hadn't broken several bones in the holidays and been replaced by the unbearable Mr Carter (alias Garters). As it is, they've just got to make the best of it – a difficult task for the dynamic Trish Moffat and her lovable but eccentric twin brother, Rocket, who's always getting into trouble; and worse still for quiet, unassuming Charlie whose famous mother just happens to be Mr Carter's favourite concert pianist . . .

Just Ferret

by Gene Kemp

Owen Hardacre, otherwise known as Ferret, can cook a casserole, pluck a chicken, mend a fuse, bake a cake, add up as fast as a calculator, do any Maths as long as it involves figures, play an accordion, draw wonderful pictures . . . but he CAN'T read, so he CAN'T write.

He's been dragged around the country by his artist father and been to so many schools that he doesn't expect much from Cricklepit Combined School. But when he makes friends with Beany and Minty and gains the respect of Sir, things begin looking up . . . even the reading!

'. . . jokes, genuine everyday drama, and surprises from the unbeatable Gene Kemp'
– *Guardian*

The Clock Tower Ghost

by Gene Kemp

Addlesbury Tower is haunted by Rich King Cole, a mean old man who fell off it long ago in mysterious circumstances. Its newest terror is Mandy – feared by her family and eventually by the ghost too. In the war they wage to dominate the tower, Mandy and King Cole do frightful and funny things to each other, little guessing how much they really have in common.

Jason Bodger and the Priory Ghost

by Gene Kemp

When Jason Bodger, school menace and student teacher's nightmare, visits a priory with Class 4Z, he has a most peculiar and disturbing experience. He sees a strange girl walking towards him high up on a non-existent beam. Mathilda de Chetwynde, born in a castle over 700 years ago, has decided that Jason is just the person she's been waiting for – and there's not a thing Jason can do about it! A hilarious, riotous tale in which the twentieth century meets the Middle Ages!

Puffin Book
of
Ghosts and Ghouls

Stories chosen by Gene Kemp

So you don't believe in ghosts? Or in ghouls, spooks and spectres? Then read on!

This chilling collection of fourteen short stories stretches out an icy hand to lead you into the disturbing world of the supernatural. Encounter the gentle but bizarre ghosts of a puppy – and a cat! Chill at the vision of the ghost of a Victorian child with disturbing powers, or shudder at two very much alive children with a gruesome plan. All of the stories here – told by distinguished authors including Philippa Pearce, Penelope Lively, Robert Westall and Gene Kemp herself – explore an unnervingly unexpected aspect of the paranormal. Each makes the unexplainable and unbelievable *so* real it will scare you witless.

So you *still* don't believe in ghosts? Read on!

The Wacky World of Wesley Baker

by Gene Kemp

'I intend to donate a cup, and I expect you to win it, my boy! . . . We're going to start a whole new programme . . . A WESLEY THE WINNER programme!'

Wesley's life is hard enough as it is. All his family are fitness freaks, while he would prefer to write stories in peace. And Agnes Potter Higgins, the maddest girl in the school, is in love with him and follows him EVERYWHERE! But when Dad decides that Wesley will be the sports day champion and Mrs Warble casts him as St George in the school play (with Agnes as the princess), his world really begins to turn upside down.

'No one writes with more insight into the primary school classroom, its pupils or its teachers than this author' – *The Irish Times*

The Well

by Gene Kemp

A secret hideaway, dragons in the well, broken vases and hidden Easter eggs: these are just some of the vivid memories which Annie Sutton (alias Gene Kemp) recalls in these perceptive tales of childhood. Living in a Midlands village in the years before the Second World War with her parents, her much-loved brother Tom and three grown-up sisters, Annie finds life full of surprises and fears, disappointments and delights.

READ MORE IN PUFFIN

For children of all ages, Puffin represents quality and variety – the very best in publishing today around the world.

For complete information about books available from Puffin – and Penguin – and how to order them, contact us at the appropriate address below. Please note that for copyright reasons the selection of books varies from country to country.

On the world wide web: www.penguin.co.uk

In the United Kingdom: Please write to *Dept. EP, Penguin Books Ltd, Bath Road, Harmondsworth, West Drayton, Middlesex UB7 ODA*

In the United States: Please write to *Consumer Sales, Penguin USA, P.O. Box 999, Dept. 17109, Bergenfield, New Jersey 07621-0120.* VISA and MasterCard holders call 1-800-253-6476 to order Penguin titles

In Canada: Please write to *Penguin Books Canada Ltd, 10 Alcorn Avenue, Suite 300, Toronto, Ontario M4V 3B2*

In Australia: Please write to *Penguin Books Australia Ltd, P.O. Box 257, Ringwood, Victoria 3134*

In New Zealand: Please write to *Penguin Books (NZ) Ltd, Private Bag 102902, North Shore Mail Centre, Auckland 10*

In India: Please write to *Penguin Books India Pvt Ltd, 706 Eros Apartments, 56 Nehru Place, New Delhi 110 019*

In the Netherlands: Please write to *Penguin Books Netherlands bv, Postbus 3507, NL-1001 AH Amsterdam*

In Germany: Please write to *Penguin Books Deutschland GmbH, Metzlerstrasse 26, 60594 Frankfurt am Main*

In Spain: Please write to *Penguin Books S. A., Bravo Murillo 19, 1° B, 28015 Madrid*

In Italy: Please write to *Penguin Italia s.r.l., Via Felice Casati 20, I–20124 Milano*

In France: Please write to *Penguin France S. A., 17 rue Lejeune, F–31000 Toulouse*

In Japan: Please write to *Penguin Books Japan, Ishikiribashi Building, 2–5–4, Suido, Bunkyo-ku, Tokyo 112*

In South Africa: Please write to *Longman Penguin Southern Africa (Pty) Ltd, Private Bag X08, Bertsham 2013*